ONE

From her spot on the nearly empty bleachers, Will Vandom watched as her teammates swam back and forth across the Heatherfield Pool.

Lean arms sliced through blue water. Sinewy legs kicked with effort. One swimmer had clearly pulled ahead of the pack, apparently unbothered by the lengthy workout. "Laura's really something," Will said, glancing at the girl sitting next to her.

The girl, Mandy Anderson, nodded. "So's Mr. Deplersun." She inclined her head of long, dark hair down toward where their muscular coach was conducting another tough practice.

"Come on! Keep going! One more lap!" the coach bellowed to the swimmers.

His deep voice echoed beneath the building's glass dome as he paced the length of the Olympic-size pool.

"He hasn't stopped shouting since I got here," Mandy laughed. "What a great set of lungs."

"No kidding," Will replied. "Coach must have been a real champ when he was younger." She smoothed her damp red bangs and stretched her arms above her head. Her hair and skin still smelled of chlorine, but she didn't mind. The tangy scent was familiar and comforting.

Practice was almost over for the evening, and Will and Mandy had finished their laps in record time. They'd already toweled off and changed into sweats. Now they were sitting in the empty bleachers, watching the other girls finish their workouts while trying to learn new techniques.

If there was one thing Will *totally* loved, it was gliding through the water. It made her feel powerful and free. It was *almost* as cool as taking down a bad guy or saving the world in her Guardian role.

Of course, Will thought, turning to look at

W.i.t.c.h.

Will Irma Taranee Cornelia Hay Lin

Friends Forever

Adapted by ALICE ALFONSI

HYPERION PAPERBACKS FOR CHILDREN
New York

© 2007 Disney Enterprises, Inc.

W.I.T.C.H. Will Irma Taranee Cornelia Hay Lin is a trademark of Disney Enterprises, Inc.

For information address Hyperion Paperbacks for Children, 114 Fifth Avenue, New York, New York 10011-5690.

Printed in the United States of America
First Edition
1 3 5 7 9 10 8 6 4 2

This book is set in 12/16.5 Hiroshige Book.
ISBN-13: 978-1-4231-0290-8
ISBN-10: 1-4231-0290-8
Visit www.clubwitch.com

I FEEL SO BAD ABOUT HOW I REACTED. MANDY AND MATT ARE JUST FRIENDS. BUT I WAS SO MEAN TO HER, AND SHE'S GOING THROUGH A REALLY ROUGH TIME . . .

HER PARENTS ARE GETTING DIVORCED, WHICH IS NEVER EASY. I SHOULD KNOW . . . I'VE BEEN THROUGH IT MYSELF.

SPEAKING OF WHICH, HOW HAVE THINGS BEEN WITH YOUR DAD BACK IN TOWN?

NOT GOOD. MOM IS REALLY UPSET. I JUST WISH SHE WOULD GIVE DAD A CHANCE.

AWEEEE-OOOO

?

!

WHAT IS *THAT*?

IT'S THE SCHOOL'S NEW PA SYSTEM. ISN'T IT GREAT? IT WAS MY IDEA TO SET IT UP.

GOOD MORNING, STUDENTS. THIS IS YOUR PRINCIPAL SPEAKING. I HAVE AN IMPORTANT ANNOUNCEMENT TO MAKE.

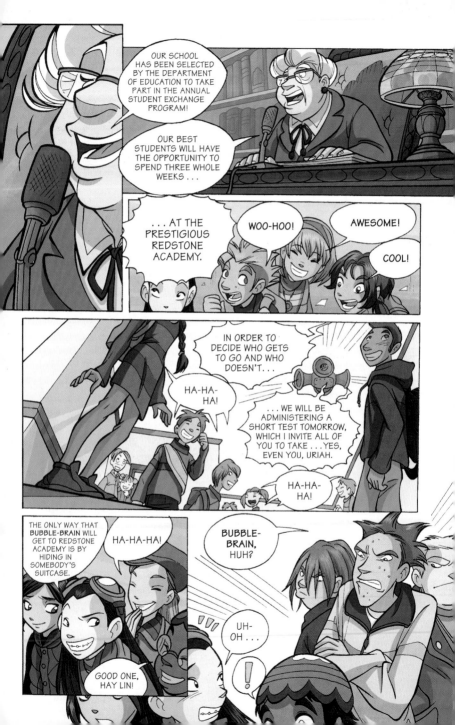

the girl beside her, she couldn't tell Mandy about the whole Guardian/save-the-universe thing. In fact, she couldn't tell *anyone*—not even her mom.

Being a Guardian was a secret Will could share only with the other members of W.I.T.C.H.—the name the five friends had given themselves by combining the initials of their first names. Besides Will, there were Irma, Taranee, Cornelia, and Hay Lin.

It's funny, Will thought, how normal that part of my life seems to me now. But that doesn't mean I can just turn to Mandy and start talking about the Oracle and Candracar, or about the Heart and the elemental powers of my four best friends. Talk about really throwing someone for a loop!

After all, even *I* could barely deal when I first found out about my powers!

It hadn't been all that long ago. Will had just moved to Heatherfield with her mom and was about to attend her first day of school. She had been supernervous as her mother dropped her off—*late*, of course—in front of Sheffield's main entrance. Will had rushed through the rain and into the big building, feeling awkward, alone, and damp.

Then she had heard a voice that changed everything.

"Two days ago, I had the same look on my face." The voice belonged to Taranee Cook, another girl new to town. The two were just getting to know each other when they saw the big gray beehive hairdo of the principal, Mrs. Knickerbocker, coming right at them. "Miss Vandom," she bellowed, "we're off to a bad start!"

Luckily, the day had ended on a much better note. Through Taranee, Will had also met Irma, Cornelia, and Hay Lin. The five girls hadn't known it at the time, but they were *destined* to be a team. It was Hay Lin's grandmother, Yan Lin, who'd explained it all to them . . . or, at least, she had *tried* to!

One afternoon shortly after, the five girls had gotten together for tea. They had been hanging out and chatting in the living room when the old woman had started talking about ancient magic, forces of good and evil, a place called the Temple of Candracar in the heart of infinity . . . all sorts of wild stuff. None of the girls truly understood everything Yan Lin had said. At least, not at first.

Now, though, the girls understood. Now they knew that the universe was made up of worlds populated by all sorts of strange creatures. And they knew that the Oracle watched over *all* those worlds from the Temple of Candracar. As Guardians, it was the girls' job to help him. Whenever evil threatened to overwhelm good, they were called upon to act.

They also now knew that, separately, their respective powers over water, fire, earth, and air weren't so strong. Which was where Will came in. She was the Keeper of the Heart of Candracar. Inside that ancient crystal lived a dazzling energy. Whenever Will summoned it, the Heart magnified the girls' separate powers, uniting them into an awesome force.

Unfortunately, Will thought now, carrying the Heart hadn't always been so awesome. The pressure of holding that much power and responsibility had strained almost every one of her relationships. Over the past year, she'd had fights with her mother and trouble in school. And at the moment, her boyfriend (if she could

even call him that anymore) was no longer talking to her.

But through it all, W.I.T.C.H. had stood by
her. The other girls had never stopped believing
in her, and they had *never* let her down.

Will was still amazed at how much she'd
been through with the other Guardians, and
how long ago those early days seemed. She'd
gotten much better at being able to balance her
two lives, and most days she felt like just an
average girl. For example, today, Will felt like
any other swimmer on Coach Deplersun's
team.

Well, maybe not like just *any* other swimmer, Will thought with a little smile. After all,
Will was one of the team's top performers. As
good as she was, however, Mandy was better.

"Are you nervous about next week's meet?"
Will asked, turning to her teammate.

Mandy's face grew tense, and her eyes
became sad. "Well, my mom's coming to watch
me," she said. "And that's making me nervous."

Will frowned. She hated to see Mandy so
down. The two girls hadn't been friends for
very long, but they were quickly becoming
close, probably because they had so much in

common. Both of them were freestyle stars. And both had parents who were dealing with marriage troubles: Mandy's parents were just starting the process of divorce, while Will's had been separated for years. The one big difference? Mandy's father had continued to be around while Will's had just reemerged in her life after a long absence.

"Things have gotten a little better," Mandy continued. "Mom doesn't get so angry now when I see my dad. And he's accepted the idea of spending less time with me."

"The important thing is to make the most of your time together," Will said, sounding wiser than she felt. "Every moment that passes is a moment that's gone forever."

Just then, Coach Deplersun blew his whistle, indicating that practice was over. The other swimmers finished their laps and began climbing out of the pool, while Will and Mandy picked up their gym bags and headed for the exit.

Mandy stopped near the doors and glanced out through the windows. The twilight sky outside had turned a dismal black. Clouds had formed above the surrounding skyscrapers, and rain was beginning to fall. Fat droplets streaked down the building's large windows. Looking over, Will noticed that Mandy's expression was as gloomy as the weather.

"If I had an eternity in front of me," Mandy said softly, "I could dedicate myself as much as I wanted to the people I love."

"That'd be nice," Will agreed. "Time is a big problem. I feel like we always end up wasting it on useless things and forget about what really counts in life."

A burst of thunder startled the girls, and Will's gaze once again moved to the giant wall of windows.

I hope I follow my own advice, Will thought. There are so many people and things in my life that I count on—my friends, my family. It's hard for me to admit that I need them, but after everything I've been through, I know that I definitely do.

Will's thoughts drifted to her father. When she was very young, he had left home. He hadn't just separated from Will's mom; he'd severed all ties with her as well. No phone calls. No letters. Not even a birthday card. *Nothing*. He'd missed seeing Will grow up over the years.

What a waste for us both, Will thought.

Then one night, he'd suddenly come back. He'd just shown up at their apartment door bearing gifts and an apology. Now that he was back in her life, Will was beginning to understand just how much she'd missed him.

Unfortunately, there was also someone else she missed these days. Matt Olsen. The boy she really liked, the boy she had fallen for, now refused to talk to her or even acknowledge her existence, and it was tearing her up inside.

She'd had a crush on him for a long time, ever since the school's Halloween dance a year before. When Will had seen his shaggy brown hair and strong, scruffy profile, she had thought he was the absolute hottest boy walking the planet.

Of course, she was smart enough to know that just because a guy was *hot* didn't mean he was *cool*! He could easily have been a total jerk.

But Matt was the opposite of a jerk. When they'd finally met, a few days after the dance, his big, brown, puppy-dog eyes were filled with laughter, and he seemed genuinely kind.

His nice-guy status had been confirmed

when he helped her rescue a little dormouse from a gang of bullies. Matt had lent her his orange sweater to wrap the little creature up in and had told her how to care for it. Since he worked in his grandfather's pet shop, Matt knew just what to do.

After that, Will and Matt had started hanging out together and talking all the time. They'd gone out on dates, too. It had been a bit overwhelming, but the rush she got when they were together was well worth it.

But then the stress of being the Keeper began to take its toll. Will had wanted to be completely open and honest with Matt, but her secret life as a Guardian always stood between them. She worried that by telling him too much, she risked losing him forever.

And then, Will had lost him anyway. Her astral drop—one of the magical doubles the Guardians created in emergency situations—had seen Matt hugging Mandy! Will had jumped to the conclusion that they were more than just friends. In her defense, it wasn't really such a crazy thing to think. Years earlier, in kindergarten, Matt and Mandy *had* been boyfriend and girlfriend, but they had long since broken up. Will, however, didn't know that. To her, it seemed as though there was *still* something going on, and she was completely enraged. She was convinced that Matt had been playing with her emotions. So, when Matt finally introduced Mandy to her, Will totally lost it.

Shouting terrible things at him, Will had ripped into Matt, yelling at him for assuming she wanted to be friends with Mandy. She'd treated him horribly, even calling him a coward.

Matt didn't react to Will's outburst. He didn't shout back. In fact, he didn't say much of anything. He just stood there, stunned and miserable, taking all of her abuse. Then he walked away. It was only later that Will found out the truth—that they were just close friends and nothing more. But by then it was too late.

Will had totally messed up, and Matt was deep in silent mode. It seemed that her "sorry" wouldn't cut it.

Thinking back on it, Will sighed. Matt wasn't just a crush; he was a friend. And it hurt to have him out of her life.

"The problem is," Will now told Mandy, "we

often realize how important someone is to us only when they're not around anymore."

Mandy studied Will's face. "Do you mean in general?" she asked. "Or are you talking about Matt?"

Will's eyes widened. "I . . . um . . . I . . ." she stammered.

"You still think about Matt, don't you?" Mandy asked.

Only *all* the time, Will thought but was too embarrassed to say out loud. Instead, she swallowed hard and babbled, "Oh, don't get me wrong! I . . . um—"

Mandy cut her off. "Will, you're making things way more complicated than they need to be. . . . You like Matt, don't you?"

"Well . . ." Will stalled, tucking a lock of bright red hair around her ear. "He's . . . he's someone I really care about."

"There's nothing wrong in *saying* that." Mandy put a hand on Will's shoulder. "I *totally* understand you. I've known Matt my whole life, and I know what a great guy he is. You shouldn't be scared to talk to him."

"But I was *so* horrible to him," Will confessed. "Now I want to make things right, tell him I thought that you and he . . . I just want to explain the misunderstanding, but now he's ignoring me!"

"He's a little upset, that's true," Mandy said.

For a second, Will felt tears well up in her eyes. Embarrassed, she looked away, silently studying the water streaking the window-panes.

"Give him some time, Will," Mandy gently advised. "Little by little, he'll get closer again. You'll see."

Will shook her head. "But I can't wait any longer. When I see him show up at school every morning, it's pure torture. It's terrible. To him, it's like I don't even exist. What can I do?"

Mandy gave Will a little smile. "You want some honest advice?"

Honk! Honk!

Will looked back out the window, Mandy's offer forgotten. An expensive-looking sports car was pulling up at the pool's entrance, its horn blasting. She pushed open the glass door to the pool and looked closer. Sitting behind the wheel was her father.

"Dad!" she cried. "What are you doing here?"

"Hop in, Will!" he called. "I'll give you a ride home!"

Will nodded. She turned back to Mandy, about to apologize for dashing off.

"Go on," Mandy said before Will said a word. "I'll call you later."

"Thanks!" Will said and dashed out into the storm.

She was sorry their conversation was being cut short, but she was relieved to have a ride home. The light rain was turning into a downpour. Taking the bus home in that mess would have been less than pleasant!

And anyway, Will told herself, didn't I just tell Mandy, *"Every moment that passes is a moment that's gone forever"*? This is a great chance to spend some more of those passing moments with my dad!

TWO

Thump-thump . . . Thump-thump . . .

Inside his sports car, Thomas Vandom listened to his windshield wipers beat out a steady rhythm. By now, the drizzly rain had turned into a total downpour, and his wipers were having a hard time keeping up. The Spider's windshield was starting to look like a miniwaterfall.

Peering through the side window, Will's father watched as his daughter raced across the wide sidewalk. At the curb, she yanked open the passenger door and bounced onto the seat beside him. A gust of wet wind swept through the interior of the car.

"Hi, Dad!" Will said brightly before slamming the door shut. Buckling her seat belt, she ran a hand through her damp red hair.

Except for some graying at the temples, Mr. Vandom's red hair was the exact same shade as Will's. He smiled down at his daughter. "Some storm, huh? Looked like the weather was going to hold out, but it's raining cats and dogs."

"I know. You showed up just in time," Will said gratefully.

Mr. Vandom shrugged. "After an afternoon in the pool, I thought a run in the rain would've been a bit much for you."

"Well, it's not like the rain would have *run* me into the ground," Will said with a little smile.

Mr. Vandom raised an eyebrow. "Still . . . if you'd caught a cold, you would've ended up with a *runny* nose."

"Oh, Dad!" Will said, laughing. "That is *so-o-o* bad."

With a flick of his wrist, Will's father turned the dial on the windshield wipers. The blades sped up.

Thump-thump! Thump-thump!

Mr. Vandom smiled to himself as he stepped on the gas and pulled into traffic. All joking aside, it was time to get something else running—his little plan.

When Will had finished laughing at his joke, he cleared his throat. "At least *someone* in the Vandom family has a sense of humor," he said carefully.

Will's brow wrinkled. "Huh?"

"You're not anything like that *grouch*, your mother."

He glanced over at Will, expecting her to agree with him. After all, Will's mother had been pretty moody lately. She'd made Will give back the new motor scooter he'd bought for her and was constantly yelling at him, despite his effort to do nice things for both of them. And the more they bonded, the grouchier she seemed to get.

Unfortunately for Mr. Vandom, Will didn't agree. Her cheerful face fell. "Mom's not a grouch," she said.

"Oh, yes, she is!" Mr. Vandom replied sharply. He needed Will on his side, or his plan would never work. "You saw yourself how she welcomed me. She wasn't exactly jumping for joy."

And that's an understatement, Mr. Vandom thought. When I showed up at the apartment, the woman looked ready to strangle me.

He had to stop himself from laughing out loud when he recalled how he'd interrupted her cozy little dinner. She'd been on a date with that boyfriend of hers—the history teacher at Will's school. What was his name? Oh, yes, Mr. Collins.

Will's father knew all about Mr. Collins, thanks to the private investigator he'd hired—Harvey Slimerick. The investigator had taken stacks of photos that showed Will's mother out on dates with Mr. Collins. And that was not all Slimerick had caught on tape. . . .

Earlier that very morning, Slimerick had knocked on Mr. Vandom's motel room door, carrying his latest batch of surveillance photos. But these didn't involve Mr. Collins. They showed something else: Will's mother whispering near an alley with a well-dressed African American woman. It was obvious the two were discussing secrets and didn't want to be seen. But they had been seen—and photographed—by Mr. Vandom's private eye.

"That's Theresa Cook . . . *Judge* Cook," Slimerick had informed Will's father when he showed him the photos. "She's the one assigned to your daughter's custody case."

Mr. Vandom couldn't believe his ears—or his luck.

"I was outside your wife's house," Slimerick continued. "I was keeping an eye on her, like you asked me to, when I saw Cook show up. What a lucky break, huh? An impartial judge should never be in contact with the claimants in her cases! You've got Cook in the palm of your hand. You could threaten her . . . or blackmail her, if you wanted to."

"Look, Harvey," Mr. Vandom replied. "This is exactly why people like you never get anywhere in life. You'll always be a Harvey Slimerick, right to the very end, because you don't see the real meaning *behind* this picture."

Mr. Vandom held up a few of the photos of Will's mother and Judge Cook talking.

Slimerick examined them again and shrugged. "What are you talking about?" he asked. "What more is there to see?"

"These aren't two defenseless little women, but two people preparing to fight. They've got something up their sleeve," Mr. Vandom replied, "and if we assume we're stronger than them, we've already lost."

Warning bells had gone off in Mr. Vandom's head when he'd seen those pictures. Which was why he was now making his next move, showing up at the Heatherfield Pool to pick Will up. He had to maintain the upper hand in his little war against her mother.

Mr. Vandom glanced across the car seat. Will's head was down. She appeared to be sinking into the shadows, her happy mood now all but gone.

Good, Mr. Vandom thought. *If she's vulnerable, I can use that to my advantage.*

"You know, I think your mom's mood might get worse soon," he warned his daughter.

Will glanced up. "What makes you say that?"

"Well, I was hoping we could spend your next vacation together."

Will's expression brightened. "Great! We haven't gone on a trip together for ages. Mom will be *so* happy!"

"I'm sure she *would*, Will. But what I had in mind was a vacation with just you and me . . .

for a whole week. We can go to some great place far away from this city. Anywhere you want. You pick. What do you say?"

Will glanced out the rain-streaked window. For a few blocks, the only sound was that made by the windshield wipers slapping away at the relentless rain pelting the car.

Thump-thump! Thump-thump!

Mr. Vandom turned a corner. "Soon you'll have to choose which side you're on, Will," he said, breaking the silence.

Will's head immediately whipped around. "What are you talking about?"

"You know that question people sometimes ask kids—'Who do you love more, Mom or Dad?'"

For a moment, Will appeared too stunned to respond. Then she furrowed her brow, and her body tensed. "That's a stupid question," she snapped. "How could anyone ask something like that?"

Perfect, Mr. Vandom thought, watching his daughter's panicked reaction. I want her to be confused. But I can't let her see that I'm pleased. I have to keep looking like the caring father.

"It's stupid, I know," he said soothingly. "But sooner or later, somebody might ask you just that. And then, Will, you'll have to have an answer."

Mr. Vandom was careful to keep his voice calm and his expression concerned. He didn't want Will to doubt him. Not now. Not after all of his efforts and plans.

Will frowned. "I don't want to talk about this anymore."

Mr. Vandom knew it was time to pull back. "Are you angry?" he asked, trying to sound hurt. "It was just a hypothetical question."

"No, it wasn't!" Will wouldn't look at him.

Mr. Vandom wasn't worried by his daughter's reaction. For weeks, he'd worked hard to build up the trust between them, knowing that a moment like this might occur.

He'd gone to all of her swim meets to cheer her on. And he'd taken her to her favorite places for dinner, like the Golden Diner. By now, he must have eaten a dozen triple cheeseburgers just to please Will.

But very soon, all his efforts were going to pay off. They had to! He *needed* them to if he was ever going to get the bigger fish—Will's mom.

All along, Will had been her father's key to making his estranged wife, Susan, suffer. Will had always been much more forgiving and accepting than her mother. He just needed to make sure things stayed that way.

Will's apartment was still three blocks away. Mr. Vandom thought he had more than enough time to smooth things over with his daughter. He was about to start telling her what a great vacation they would have together when Will surprised him.

"Stop the car!" she cried. "I'm getting out."

For a moment, Mr. Vandom's foot lifted off the gas pedal, but then he placed it back on. He had no intention of stopping the car. Will, however, was determined. She opened the door on her side while they were still moving.

There was nothing he could do. Will's father immediately pulled over to the curb and put the car in park. "We're not there yet, Will!" he cried. "You'll get soaking wet!"

Will didn't seem to care. She leaped out of the car, dragging her gym bag behind her.

"Will!" Mr. Vandom shouted. "Get back here!"

Slam! Will shut the door behind her and

stood in the pouring rain.

Mr. Vandom unbuckled his seat belt. He popped open his own door. "Will!" he shouted again, raising his head above the roof of the car. But his daughter ignored him, racing away into the storm.

Mr. Vandom's fists pounded the wet top of the car. *Bang!* The steady rain was soaking him, but he didn't care. He was too focused on Will.

I pushed too hard, he thought, but I'm not giving up! Not now. Not after I've come this far.

THREE

Will thought she could run fast enough to stay dry, but her apartment building was still far away. Within thirty seconds, she was drenched.

Well, she thought, I can't get any wetter. Guess there's no point in running anymore. . . .

Her pumping legs slowed, and her pink sneakers began slogging through the sidewalk puddles. As her clothes became weighed down with water, her mind filled up with questions.

"Why would he ask me to choose between him and Mom? Is he thinking of going after custody of me?" she whispered to herself. Will didn't want to believe that her father would subject her to that. After all, he was her father, and he loved her. He wouldn't want to see her get hurt, right?

"Maybe he's afraid my mom's going to bring a lawsuit against him," she whispered. "He's probably worried that *she'll* start a custody fight."

Her mother *had* been fighting with her dad since the day he'd reappeared in their lives. Even so, Will had been hoping that the two of them would work things out. Will dreamed of the day they'd all live together again—one big, happy family, in one big house! It would be perfect. Will would have two parents to love her, a backyard to play in. Yet, in the car, her dad had hinted that her beautiful dream was *not* going to come true.

"So, then, why did he come back to Heatherfield?" Will whispered to herself. "What does he want from us? And what does he want from me?"

A jagged flash of lightning ripped the dark night as the rain continued to pour down. Will barely seemed to notice. Lost in her unhappy thoughts, she continued to trudge home, dejected and confused.

By the time she reached her building, Will

was so wet that she decided against taking the elevator, fearing she would leave a giant, embarrassing puddle in it. Slowly, she climbed the stairs to her apartment.

Finally reaching her door, Will fished around inside her bag for her key. It was lost somewhere beneath all her swimming gear. Realizing that a pool of water was forming at her feet, Will gave up on finding the key and banged on the apartment door.

The sound of her fist hitting the wood reminded her of the night her dad had knocked on that very same door. She'd been so excited to see him that she hadn't stopped to think about whether or not his smile was genuine.

But after what her dad had just said in the car, she couldn't help wondering—had he really been sorry about interrupting their dinner with Mr. Collins? Had he really been glad to see her? Or, had he been happier about upsetting her mom?

She couldn't be sure. And trying to figure it all out was giving her a massive headache!

I thought I knew my dad, Will thought. But what did I ever really know about him?

"Will!" her mom cried as she finally opened

the door and saw her soaked daughter standing there.

"Hi, Mom."

Even after a long day, her mother looked perfectly put together. She was still wearing her work clothes, a silky pine-green skirt, and a delicate cream-colored blouse. Her dark hair hung in sleek waves around her face.

I can never get my own head of annoying red cowlicks to look that good, Will mused. Only when I'm transformed into a Guardian do I begin to feel as powerful, beautiful, and in control as my mom always seems to be.

"For heaven's sake!" her mom cried, gaping at Will's dripping hair and workout clothes, unaware of her daughter's inner turmoil. "What happened to you? You're drenched!"

"Everything's fine," Will mumbled. "Dad gave me a ride home."

"What, in a *speedboat*?" her mom asked.

Will didn't reply. She went straight to the bathroom and peeled off her damp sweats, throwing them into the bathtub. *Splat!*

Then she padded into her bedroom and changed into a dry tank top and pink shorts. A moment later, her mom came in with a big, fluffy towel and gently rubbed Will's wet hair until it was no long dripping. She helped Will into a warm bathrobe.

"So, seriously, honey, how did you get so wet?" she asked as they walked back out into the living room.

"Dad and I were talking, and . . ." Will shrugged, not sure how to talk about what her father had said.

For a long, silent moment, Will's mom studied her daughter's face. Then she reached for one of the papers on the coffee table.

"Did he tell you about this?" she asked softly.

Will had assumed the papers on the sofa and coffee table were part of her mom's office work. But the paper her mom held up displayed a legal seal.

Will skimmed the document. "It's a letter from the courthouse."

"I got it this morning," Will's mom said. "It's a subpoena. There's going to be a hearing about your custody."

"M—my c—custody?" Will stammered.

It was one thing for dad to *hint* about the *possibility* of a custody case, Will fumed. But it was a whole other thing to hear that it was actually happening.

Will would have been less shocked if the lightning outside had reached through the window and struck her!

"Your father wants you to live with him, Will," her mom said. "He wants to take you away from me. This is the *wonderful* man who came back to stay by his family's side!"

Will could hear the bitterness in her mom's voice. She couldn't blame her . . . and yet, Will loved her dad. She couldn't help it. In spite of everything, he was still her *dad*!

Having him around had been so amazing. For the first time, Will had been able to hear about her childhood through her dad's eyes. Whenever they had dinner together, he would tell her stories about what she had been like as a very young child. His memories were so vivid Will felt as though she were looking at pictures.

Will loved hearing those stories. In one of her favorites, she'd been no more than two, holding her father's hand as they'd walked along the sidewalk one evening.

"What's that, Daddy?" a young Will had

squealed, pointing to a bright white globe in the night sky.

"That's the moon, honey," Will's dad had replied. "Do you like it?"

"No!" little Will had cried, tugging hard on his pant leg. "Turn it off!"

The doting way her dad talked about her childhood made Will believe he really did love her and care about her.

But could he really care about me if he's doing this? Will thought. He knows I love my mom. He has to know a custody battle in court is the *last* thing I'd ever want to go through.

"I . . . I can't believe it," Will murmured. "I don't want to believe it." She met her mother's eyes. "Why would he do a thing like this?"

"That's something you'll have to ask him yourself," her mom said. "I knew he had something up his sleeve when he refused to sign the divorce papers."

"This is awful!" Will cried, shaking her head.

Will tried to imagine sitting in court and being asked to choose between her parents. Obviously, her dad thought she was going to choose him. And she was pretty sure she knew why. As Will and her father had grown closer, Will had started to tell him about the fights she'd had with her mother. And there had been plenty to talk about. Thinking about it now, Will could see how her dad might have gotten the impression she was unhappy.

From the day they'd moved to Heatherfield, Will and her mother had argued practically nonstop. At first, Will had been angry with her mom for leaving Fadden Hills. She'd relocated their lives without consulting her. And Will thought it was totally unfair!

Then her mom had started dating Will's history teacher, Mr. Collins. And the way Will found out? She had seen them—in public!—on a date. Will had been so embarrassed. She'd argued with her mom for weeks before finally realizing there was nothing she could do about the relationship.

Things didn't get much better after that. Will's duties as Keeper had become more demanding. And her mother was very busy. Between her high-pressure job at Simultech and dating Mr. Collins, Will's mother had had very little time for her. When she did, she expected Will to drop her friends and her own plans instantly. That had led to more fighting.

Then one night, just when Will had thought her mother didn't care about her at all anymore, she'd heard her call out, "Will! Can you come here for a minute?"

Will had walked into the dining room to find her mom standing over a candlelit table. The table was set with their best china and silverware—and there were only two plates.

"Where is your date?" Will had asked, her fists clenched. She knew her mom was supposed to be seeing Will's history teacher for dinner—again. Looking at the beautiful way the table was set, Will could tell she'd gone to a lot of trouble to impress him.

"If you're speaking of Mr. Collins," her mother had said, "he's not here. I postponed our date."

Then Will's mom pulled out a chair for her daughter and smiled. "Sometimes the most romantic of evenings isn't worth as much as a dinner . . . between friends."

Will had been touched by her mother's gesture and instantly stopped being so angry. They ended up having a wonderful dinner together.

From then on, things only got better. Sure, they continued to have arguments. Their ups and downs never fully went away, but now Will knew her mother really loved and cared about her.

And Will loved and trusted her mother, too. After all, *she* was the parent who'd stuck around to raise her!

Will would never *choose* to part with her mother, but then again, the choice might not end up hers to make. Anything could happen in court. Her dad might have some legal tricks up his sleeve. It could turn out that Will would *have* to live with her father. And she wasn't sure she wanted to be forced into living with him no matter how much fun he *had* been. She heaved a sigh and looked over at her mother.

Will's mom seemed totally stressed about the whole thing. She had gone over to the sofa, where she'd sat down heavily. "Come here, Will," she said softly.

As Will sat down beside her mom, the day's events finally got to her. Her own eyes began to well up, tears wetting her cheeks.

Will's mom hugged her close. "My little sweetheart!" she whispered.

The walk in the rain had chilled Will's skin. Now she clung to her mother's warmth. "I was just really hoping . . ." Will squeezed her eyes shut. "I was hoping we could all live together."

"If he told you there was any chance of that," said her mom, "he was lying."

Will's tears continued to flow. Her heart was breaking, her dreams were shattering, and she couldn't hold back the flood.

Her mom rocked her as if she were little again. For a few minutes, Will wished she really *were* little. All those years ago, she hadn't understood what her parents were going through. She'd been too young.

Now Will understood all too well what was happening, and she hated it. She hated feeling so helpless.

As the Keeper of the Heart, Will had triumphed over dark magic and evil forces. She'd vanquished horrifying creatures and ruthless monsters. But in this situation, Will simply didn't know how to fight.

For the first time in a long while, the leader of W.I.T.C.H. felt totally and completely lost.

After a few minutes of bitter crying, Will wiped her damp cheeks. She leaned far enough away from her mother to look into her face.

"So what are we going to do now?" she whispered.

Her mother took a deep breath and let it out. "There's still time. My lawyer will take care of it, but you can count on one thing . . . I'll give Thomas one heck of a battle in court."

The flash of raw ferocity in her mother's eyes surprised Will.

"I'm not going to lose you," her mother declared. "That's a promise!"

Once again, Will wrapped her arms around her mother and held on tight. Inside, she was trembling like a frightened foal. But her mother was still and calm. And that spoke louder than all the words in the world.

They would make it through—in time.

FOUR

This totally stinks, Cornelia Hale thought as she sat in her last class of the day, drumming her manicured fingernails on her desktop.

Mr. Collins was passing out a surprise test, which was totally unfair! He had always warned his classes about major quizzes and tests. But this time he'd given them zero advanced warning.

When he dropped the preprinted test on Cornelia's desk, she quickly snatched it up and glanced through the questions.

Wait a second, she thought. Mr. Collins teaches history, but this doesn't look like a history test. Then she remembered Mrs. Knickerbocker's announcement from the day before.

"Our school has been selected by the Department of Education for the annual student exchange program," the principal had said over the loudspeaker. "Our best students will spend three weeks at the prestigious Redstone Academy. Tomorrow we will begin to administer a short test . . ."

Okay, Cornelia thought, so we *were* warned about the test. I just forgot!

The test questions appeared to cover all sorts of subjects: math, spelling, grammar. Beside each question was a little row of oval boxes. The instructions said to choose just one answer per question and fill in the box with a number two pencil.

"Don't worry," Mr. Collins told his history class as he started passing out the pencils. "It's just a series of simple questions. All of your schoolmates are taking this."

As he continued to walk around the room, he explained what the results would be used for. "It's an aptitude test to understand you better," he said, "and to evaluate you with greater precision—"

Uriah snorted loudly. Cornelia glanced in his direction. Not surprisingly, the school's biggest troublemaker was giving the teacher attitude—again. He'd laced his hands behind his spiky orange hair and was smirking.

Mr. Collins ignored him. "This test will allow us to choose the finest, most suitable students to take part in Sheffield's student exchange program," he continued. "You have one hour to finish, and *no cheating*!" He glared at Uriah for a moment. "It wouldn't do you any good anyway," he added, returning the kid's smirk. Then he clapped his hands and said, "Let's get to it! Good luck, everyone!"

Okay, Cornelia thought, flipping her straight blond hair over her shoulder, let's see what we've got here. First question . . .

> Which of the following is least like
> the others?
> A. square
> B. triangle
> C. octagon
> D. circle

Cornelia smiled. Of course, the answer is *D*, she thought. The circle is round. All the other shapes have straight sides and angles.

With satisfaction, Cornelia neatly filled in the little oval beside the letter *D*. She went on to answer the second, third, and fourth questions without any problem.

This is easy! she realized. Glancing over at Will, she tried to share a triumphant smile. Unfortunately, Will was staring off into space, ignoring the paper on her desktop.

Uh-oh, Cornelia thought. Will's spacing out again.

All afternoon, Will had seemed distracted. In two of their classes, the teachers had called on her. But both times, her response had been a mumbled, "I'm sorry, I don't know. . . ."

Now, if clueless Irma had given a couple of sorry answers like that, Cornelia wouldn't have thought twice about it. But Will had a brain. She always made an effort in school.

Something's definitely off, Cornelia decided. Ever since lunch, she has been acting so strangely.

Earlier that day, the members of W.I.T.C.H. had gathered around their usual table in the cafeteria. Hay Lin, Taranee, and Irma were talking excitedly about an upcoming school dance: Hay Lin was going to work on all the decorations; Irma was still complaining about not having a boyfriend to go with; and Taranee was wondering what she could wear that her boyfriend, Nigel, hadn't seen her in yet.

Cornelia had smiled listening to her friend talk so animatedly about Nigel. She still remembered that day more than a year before, when she'd invited Taranee and Will to their first Halloween dance at Sheffield.

Taranee had been so studious and quiet. She'd had no interest in attending the dance. And she probably wouldn't have come if Cornelia hadn't pushed her to.

Things sure had changed. These days, Taranee had a steady boyfriend. She no longer gnawed nervously at her fingernails. She'd even convinced her superstrict mom that there was more to life than perfect grades.

And speaking of change, Cornelia had thought as she munched on a carrot stick, Will Vandom has certainly changed over the past year, too.

In her baggy clothes and scuffed green sneakers, Will had looked like a major tomboy the day Cornelia first laid eyes on her. Like Taranee, she'd been awkward and shy. She was constantly biting her lip and letting her mop of red hair fall into her eyes.

Will still dressed like a tomboy, although she'd added a number of cute skirts and boots to her wardrobe—like the stylish, pink and black outfit she wore today. But she definitely wasn't shy anymore. And she no longer hid from the world behind her long bangs.

Will was a leader now. She walked with confidence through the halls at school. She was bold and strong, a top-ranked freestyle swimmer, and she didn't hesitate to speak her mind. When W.I.T.C.H. needed to act, Will was ready.

All of which explained why Will's behavior was setting off alarm bells in Cornelia.

Are her troubles with Matt getting to Will? Cornelia wondered.

During lunch, the other girls hadn't seemed to notice Will's subdued mood. They had just kept right on talking and laughing. Of course, that didn't surprise Cornelia. The other girls weren't insensitive, but none of them knew what it was like to have her heart broken. Only Cornelia knew . . . and that was what had changed *her* the most over the past year.

Even before her heart was broken by him, Cornelia had dreamed of Caleb. So, when she finally met the young rebel from Meridian, she had felt as if she had known him forever.

Whenever she was with him, Cornelia had felt her spirits soar. She had been so unbelievably happy. And whenever they parted, she had missed him with an almost feverish intensity.

She had constantly daydreamed of his handsome face, fiery brown eyes, and passionate spirit. Time and again she'd admired the courageous way he had fought to free the Meridians from the rule of an evil prince. Time and again, she'd recalled his tender words and touches.

Cornelia had been sure they'd be together one day. She had wanted nothing more than for Caleb to become a permanent part of her life. Then, they'd never have had to be parted again.

But they *had* parted.

Ironically, in the end, it wasn't otherworldly forces and evil creatures that had separated Cornelia from Caleb. A few words had been all it took to break Cornelia's heart.

"I've thought about us a lot, Cornelia,"

Caleb had told her that awful day in Candracar. "You know how much I care about you. . . . You know what brings us together. And you also know the pain we've suffered."

"That pain is over, Caleb!" Cornelia had assured him. "None of the people who've hurt us can harm us anymore!"

And it was true. Prince Phobos, Caleb's enemy, had been defeated. And the Guardians had completely stopped the evil sorceress Nerissa from destroying Candracar. The bad guys had been vanquished. It was time to relax!

Caleb was now free to join Cornelia in Heatherfield. Nothing should have stood between her and the boy of her dreams, except that something did . . . *the boy of her dreams himself*!

After all they'd been through together, and after all Cornelia had risked to save him and bring him back to life, Caleb had simply changed his mind about her.

"I've thought it over," he'd continued, "and I'm going back to Meridian. For your own good, for our own good, I'm not going to ask you to come with me."

"You're . . . you're leaving me?" Cornelia

cried in shock. "Breaking up with me? *Dumping* me? Without giving me any say in the matter?"

"Try to understand," Caleb explained. "You and I are just too different."

"No, I don't understand!" Cornelia shouted back. "Why are you talking to me like this? Why are you telling me these things?"

"This . . . this isn't what you really look like," he countered. "I fell in love with somebody who doesn't exist. . . ."

Cornelia couldn't believe her ears. She'd thought they were soul mates. She'd thought they shared a deep connection that could never be broken. But Caleb was acting no differently than some shallow high school boy freaked out by a girlfriend's zit!

The boy from Meridian had broken up with her because she'd finally shown herself to him—in her normal, human form. He saw the girl she really was beneath her dazzling earth Guardian image. And he couldn't handle it. He thought she was too weak . . . too human . . . to share a life with him on another world.

"I'm disappointed, Caleb," she said. "I thought you were different, but I was wrong. You're . . . you're a total *worm*!"

And with that, it was over, done. The searing pain of that realization had ripped through Cornelia worse than anything she'd ever experienced.

Only one thing had kept her from crumbling completely . . . her best friends. She ran to them crying and collapsed right into their arms. They had hugged her, comforted her, and let her cry.

When the tears had finally stopped flowing, the world no longer looked the same to Cornelia. She'd finally realized how much time and energy she'd wasted over the past year, daydreaming about Caleb.

Obsessing over Caleb for so long had narrowed Cornelia's vision. Now her eyes had been opened again, and she began to notice things she'd never seen before—like the homeless man in the park, the night she'd come back from saving Candracar.

The old Cornelia would have walked right by the poor, shivering man. The new Cornelia, however, used her magic to grow him a wonderful shelter of branches, vines, and leaves.

And she began to notice other things,

too. . . . For example, she started noticing when her mom was feeling down, or when her little sister was sad.

And today, she'd noticed right away that something was not right with Will.

Cornelia had planned to wait until after school to ask Will what was wrong . . . until she saw her spacing out in history class. The questions on the test were easy. But Will wasn't even *trying*. Her chin was propped in her hands as though she didn't have the energy to keep her head up without help. The corners of her mouth were turned down in a frown. And her eyes were staring off into thin air!

"Will?" Cornelia whispered across the aisle. "Will?"

Will blinked and shook her head, as if Cornelia had called her back from another dimension.

Cornelia glanced quickly toward the front of the room to make sure Mr. Collins wasn't looking in their direction. He wasn't. The teacher was busy grading a stack of students' papers.

Cornelia turned back to Will. "What's the matter?" she quietly demanded. "Why aren't you writing?"

"I was thinking about my dad. . . ." Will admitted. She shook her head and sighed. "I thought he was a different person."

Quietly, Will explained that her dad was suing for sole custody of her, and that he was making her choose between him and her mom.

"What did your mom say?" Cornelia whispered.

"She told me not to worry," Will said with a shrug, "but I couldn't sleep all night."

No kidding! Cornelia thought. If that were happening to me, I'd be a total wreck! She glanced at her wristwatch. Forty minutes more and this stupid test will be over, she thought. School will be over, too. Then I can find Irma, Taranee, and Hay Lin, and we can all help Will sort out this mess.

That's what being a part of W.I.T.C.H. means, Cornelia thought. No matter what the universe throws at us, we don't have to face it alone!

FIVE

BRRRIIIIINGGGG!

Hay Lin smiled when she heard the last bell of the day. *Free again*, she sang to herself, *at least until tomorrow!*

She rose from her desk and turned in her test. Some of the questions had been easy, some less so. Hay Lin figured she had done okay overall, but now that it was over, she wasn't going to stress out about it.

As she walked into the crowded hallway, Hay Lin smoothed the back of her head for about the hundredth time that day. Her long, blue-black hair fell loosely down her back and swayed with her steps.

Hay Lin almost always wore her hair the same way—in two

long pigtails tied tightly at the nape of her neck. Today, however, she'd decided to try a style that made her look, and feel, a little older than the little-girl pigtails did.

In the shower that morning, she had used a special conditioner. She blew her hair dry and brushed it out. Then she tried her new ceramic styling iron on it. Now her superstraight locks fell in a glossy curtain, curling just a little bit at the ends. As she caught a glimpse of her reflection in a glass door, Hay Lin's smile grew wider. She had to admit, she was liking the new look—a lot.

Today's outfit wasn't bad, either. She wore a new, baby blue, off-the-shoulder blouse. And, around the hips of her vintage jeans, she'd slung a loose yellow belt with a buckle in the shape of a star.

Eric had actually tripped when he'd seen her in the school courtyard earlier that morning. Hay Lin had giggled, seeing her boyfriend lose his cool like that. After he regained his balance, he'd walked up to her, his brown eyes wide, and said, "Wow! You look great!"

Her reply was a beaming, braces-filled grin. Most girls would have been shy about a mouth full of metal, but Hay Lin didn't care. In fact, she liked showing her braces off. She'd designed them herself, using W.I.T.C.H.'s elemental symbols. So why not be proud of them?

Unfortunately, bullies like Uriah and his friends did not see her braces as a thing of beauty. "Metal Mouth" continued to be Uriah's favorite put-down for her. Hay Lin had used to feel pretty defenseless against Uriah and his mean words, but over the past year, W.I.T.C.H. had faced off against some of the nastiest supernatural creatures in the universe. In comparison, Uriah and his pals weren't that big a deal.

Plus, how could she take seriously a put-down from a boy who looked as if his head were on fire?

Spotting Taranee opening the locker next to hers, Hay Lin thought, maybe I should ask Taranee if she ever considered *setting* Uriah's hair on fire.

After greeting the fire Guardian, Hay Lin spun the combination on her own locker and popped open the door. As she started pulling out books, Irma walked up to the two girls.

"Stupid exam!" Irma complained loudly.

A few kids passing by looked their way at the sound of Irma's loud voice. Hay Lin glanced at Taranee, and both girls rolled their eyes. Water girl was never one to hold back the flow!

"That exam was just another excuse to torture us!" Irma went on, pretending to tear out her short brown hair. "What good were all those questions, anyhow?"

"It was a sort of IQ test," Taranee calmly explained. "The principal wants to look good to the Department of Education. After all, a high grade point average isn't always an indication of gray matter."

"What do you mean, grade point average?" Irma demanded. "School just started!"

"But you have a GPA on file," Taranee pointed out, adjusting her round glasses.

"Oh, I get it," Irma said. "They're going to look at our grades from last year."

Hay Lin laughed and tossed her gleaming dark hair. "If that's the case, then I don't have a very good chance of getting into the exchange program."

Clang!

A boy's large and very freckled hand had

slammed shut Hay Lin's locker door, almost hitting her in the nose!

"If you want, I can give you a lift," the boy said to Hay Lin in a nasty tone. "If we squeeze in tight, there's room for both of us in my suitcase."

Uriah! Hay Lin groaned silently.

She wasn't all that surprised to see the bully up close and personal. In fact, she was pretty sure she knew exactly why he'd stopped by to mess with her.

The day before, she'd referred to him as "Bubble-brain" in the school hallway. She honestly hadn't meant for him to overhear the insult, but he had. Now he was here to get a little revenge.

Hay Lin gulped nervously as she turned around. The boy might be a ridiculous combination of zits and hair gel, but he was still a scary thug—especially when he was *this* close! He'd even brought his brain-dead posse to help frighten her. Chubby Kurt stood on his right. Big, blond, buzz-cut Laurent stood on his left. And all three boys looked ready for trouble.

"Uriah!" Hay Lin exclaimed in a saccharine voice. "What a pleasant surprise!"

Uriah poked her shoulder. "Your little wise-crack yesterday wasn't very funny, Miss Metal Mouth."

"Oh? Did that *bother* you?" Hay Lin asked, trying not to let the cruel nickname get under her skin. "But I was only kidding!"

Suddenly Irma stepped forward. "That's right!" she said, putting her hands on her hips. "So why don't you give it a break, Uriah, and go pick on someone else?"

"Well, how about this? Why don't *you* take a hike?" Uriah hissed. He glared at Irma and then at Taranee, who was scowling behind Irma. "I need to have a chat with my little friend here."

Hay Lin glanced up and down the hallway. No teachers were in sight to save the day. And Eric wasn't around, either.

That's probably just as well, thought Hay Lin. Last time Uriah picked on me, Eric was around, and the results weren't pretty.

It had happened the night they'd gone on a sort of double date with Taranee and Nigel to the Rock and Roll Café. The date had turned bad when Uriah showed up, and Eric tried to defend Hay Lin's honor after Uriah went after her.

It had been sweet of Eric to step up, but, in

the end, Hay Lin and Taranee were the ones who'd taken care of Uriah and his gang. With a little air magic, Hay Lin had blown Uriah down the street! And Taranee's firepower had given Kurt the hotfoot!

Thinking about that night, Hay Lin couldn't help smiling. She really liked Eric. He was a good and supportive guy. Supersmart *and* supercute! But Hay Lin also knew what made her strong, and it wasn't Eric Lyndon.

When Hay Lin's life got rocky at home or in school, it was her best friends who had always been there for her.

Having a boyfriend was great, but she had seen what happened to Cornelia. Boyfriends *could* let you down. But no matter what, the members of W.I.T.C.H. would always be there for each other—like right now!

Standing in front of Hay Lin's locker, Uriah believed he had the upper hand. But he didn't. Not with Irma and Taranee right there, watching Hay Lin's back.

"You're going to apologize for what you called me, Metal Mouth!" Uriah barked, pointing his grubby finger at her.

"Why should I have to apologize for saying

'bubble-brain'?" Hay Lin asked. Just for fun, she made sure to say "bubble-brain" extra loud.

Uriah's smirk disappeared. His eyes widened in outrage. "Don't say that again!" Uriah shouted. "I don't want to hear you say that word!"

The angrier Uriah got, the more Hay Lin grinned. She scratched her head as if she were confused. "So tell me," she said in a clueless voice, "if I can be Metal Mouth, why can't you be Bubble-brain?"

"You're doing this on purpose! You're trying to make fun of me!" Like a toddler having a tantrum, Uriah stamped his foot in its dirty sneaker. Then he reached past Hay Lin, opened her locker door, and turned to his large, lumpy friend.

"Empty out her locker, Kurt!" he commanded. "Clown Girl's got to understand that she's fooling with the wrong guy!"

Kurt cracked his knuckles and smirked. "My pleasure, Uriah."

"No!" Taranee roared.

Before Kurt could take one step forward, Taranee slammed Hay Lin's locker door shut with a loud bang!

Fists clenched, Taranee stepped up and glared at Kurt and Uriah. "You can't just do whatever you want," she warned them.

"Oooh, I'm scared," Uriah taunted. "Should we leave, guys?"

Kurt and Laurent laughed. Uriah sneered. Then they all started moving toward the girls, fists raised.

Irma leaned toward Taranee, "Shouldn't we try *not* to make them angry?" she whispered.

"Get out of here right now!" Taranee warned the boys, ignoring Irma's remark, "or I'll tell the principal!"

The thugs continued to close in.

This is not good, Hay Lin thought as Uriah's face loomed closer. Not good at all.

SIX

Just when it looked like there was no escape, Will's voice called out, "If I were you, I'd take Taranee's advice."

"And *quick*, too," Cornelia added.

Hay Lin looked up and smiled in relief. Reinforcements had arrived! The two girls were standing a few feet away. Will's arms were folded, and her eyes were locked onto Uriah, while Cornelia stood with her hands on her hips. Her glare looked lethal.

Uriah appeared surprised for a second. Then he recovered, and his nasty sneer broadened.

"Looks like someone's temper is getting a little too hot," Will remarked.

"You don't say! Well, I think this

calls for a fire extinguisher!" Uriah announced. He walked over to the cherry-red can and pulled it off the wall.

"Uh-oh!" Hay Lin cried as he aimed the fire extinguisher's nozzle straight at Will and Cornelia.

"Ha-ha-ha!" Uriah cackled as he pulled the pin and depressed the handle, sending a cloud of white foam pouring out of the nozzle.

Cornelia and Will jumped backward.

"Aaargh!" Cornelia cried in outrage.

The earth Guardian's eyes narrowed, and Hay Lin smiled. She could only guess what Cornelia had in store for Uriah!

With Cornelia's power over rocks, plants, and trees, she could command the bricks in the wall to drop down and form a wall around the bullies. Or maybe she would make the potted plants down the hall reach out their limbs, wrap them around the boys' ankles, and drag them straight into the principal's office, where they belonged.

Hay Lin could hardly wait to see what was going to happen next!

And it didn't look as though she'd have to wait long.

Cornelia lifted her palm and aimed it at Uriah's spiky head. "I'm going to—"

"No, Cornelia!" Will cried, lunging to pull the girl's arm down. Then, under her breath, she hissed, "We can't use our powers here!"

Cornelia was obviously still angry, but Will's words seemed to sink in. Slowly, she began to lower her arm. "Then what are we going to do?" she whispered back.

Hay Lin saw Will glance at Uriah, Kurt, and Laurent, then at her friends. She knew what the Keeper was thinking. Without their powers, it would be hard to stand up to the bullies. There really was only one choice.

"Run!" Will cried, and then they took off.

It took Uriah a second to register that all five girls were in motion. "Let's get them, guys!" he shouted, and the boys were off in pursuit.

Hay Lin raced down the hall behind Will, Cornelia, and Irma, with Taranee right behind her.

As they turned the corner, Hay Lin glanced back. She wanted to see how close Uriah and his friends were getting. But Taranee pushed her forward. "Just keep moving!" she warned.

Will quickly led the girls down the long

hallway and around another corner.

"Thanks for the help, by the way!" Irma said sarcastically, her words aimed at Will.

Will ignored her. Instead, she addressed Cornelia. "What were you thinking of doing?" she asked. "Transforming them? Zapping them in the behinds?"

Hay Lin frowned as she ran. She knew it was against the Guardian rules to use their powers for trivial stuff. But that didn't mean that every once in a while it wasn't okay to bend those rules. She'd done it before—outside the Rock and Roll Café, when she'd blown Uriah back down the street.

Okay, she admitted to herself, so the police had come, and she'd spent a few too many hours in the station house. But she still didn't think using a little magic was a big deal—especially for a cause as worthy as smacking Uriah down!

As if reading Hay Lin's thoughts, Will spoke up. "We're in school, in case you haven't noticed!" the Keeper of the Heart firmly reminded them all. "And we have to act like everybody else here!"

Well, I guess we're following orders, Hay

Lin thought as they continued sprinting down the hallway, because in case Will hasn't noticed, we *are* acting like everyone else—we're running *away* from Uriah.

W.I.T.C.H. turned one more corner and found themselves near a side exit. An escape! But when Will tried the door, it was locked.

Uh-oh, Hay Lin thought. This is not good.

The thudding thunder of boys' sneakers was growing closer. Suddenly, the three rounded the corner.

"There they are!" Laurent bellowed from the other end of the hall.

"Come on!" Will cried.

The girls followed Will down another short hallway. But there was nowhere to go from there. It was a dead end. Then Hay Lin noticed a wooden door marked PRIVATE. Will had apparently seen it as well, and was leading them right to it.

"The janitor's closet," Will said, opening the door. "Inside! Quick!"

The closet was small and dark and smelled like a pair of old, wet socks. Nevertheless, the girls quickly crowded in, and Will shut the door.

In the dim light, Hay Lin made out shelves of cleaning fluids. Brooms and mops stood in buckets on the floor, their wooden handles sticking out in different directions. The girls squeezed further into the room and crouched down. It felt as if they were hiding among the tall reeds of a funky-smelling swamp!

Hay Lin heard sounds in the hallway, outside the door. First came running footsteps. Then came the puffing and panting sounds of boys breathing hard. Hay Lin tried not to giggle. Uriah and his crew probably weren't prepared for sprinting after the athletic Guardians!

The doorknob began to rattle, and Hay Lin stifled a gasp. This was it. They were in real trouble now.

"Mr. Sylla!" Hay Lay heard Uriah call out as the knob stopped rattling.

Hmmm, she sighed in relief, *our new computer science teacher must be nearby. I wonder if he saw us go into this closet.*

"Well, actually I . . ." Uriah was saying.

Hay Lin didn't hear anything else. Irma, who was crouched right beside her, chose that moment to start talking.

"You've had better ideas, Will!" she whispered in a freaked-out voice. "What do we do now?"

Will didn't miss a beat. "We get out of here," she quietly declared, "and fast."

"But how?" Hay Lin asked.

Will paused before answering. "With transposition! You know it works."

Hay Lin smiled. Transposition, she thought. Of course!

"Perfect!" Cornelia whispered. "We can beam ourselves out of the school without getting caught by Uriah and his pals!"

The Guardians had resorted to transposition several times before to go from one place to the other. Hay Lin still remembered the wild ride she and Will had taken from Heatherfield to Fadden Hills to visit the former Guardian Kadma. They'd used their mental projections and the power of the Heart to travel through space. It had worked then, so Hay Lin was sure it would work now.

Will closed her eyes and stretched her hands out in front of her. She extended the index finger of each hand, holding one inches above the other. In the empty space between her two fingers, a light appeared. It was the Heart of Candracar.

Dazzling pink energy pulsed inside the shadows of the closet. The supernatural light cast a glow upon each of the Guardians' faces.

"Okay," Will whispered, calling up a small piece of the Heart's infinite power. "Concentrate. Think hard about your final destination."

Hay Lin stared into the bright pink light and thought about her home above the Silver Dragon restaurant. Inside the second-floor apartment, her bedroom was waiting for her. She pictured it as she'd left it that morning. There were drawings and colored pencils scattered all over. Clothes were thrown haphazardly on the bed and floor.

Hay Lin looked around. The other girls had closed their eyes. The pink light between Will's fingers grew brighter and brighter.

Hay Lin was a little nervous, but she was excited, too. She closed her eyes to concentrate better. Then she pictured her bedroom again and envisioned herself arriving there. As she did, she felt a tingling energy surround her entire body.

She focused even harder, and the energy

seemed to lift her up. Suddenly, a lightning-bright flash penetrated her closed eyelids, and—

Shaaaaa-zaaatz!

The foul-smelling closet was gone.

SEVEN

Shaaaaa-zaaatz!

Will opened her eyes to find herself standing in the middle of her bedroom. "Wow!"

Squeak! Squeak! Squeak!

Will's pet dormouse was jumping nervously up and down on her bed. Her sudden arrival had scared the poor thing!

Will smiled and cooed, "It's just me, dormouse. Don't worry."

The furry little creature quickly calmed down and scampered over to her, and she petted its soft fur and scratched behind its ears.

Transposition is so awesome, she thought as she tried to calm the dormouse down. It's like traveling on a lightning bolt across the sky.

"I should use that trick more often," she told her pet with a laugh. "It sure saves time walking home!"

She picked her dormouse up and gave it a kiss. Then she placed it back on the bed and headed toward the door. It was a good thing only the dormouse was home, Will thought as she turned the knob, because it would have been hard to explain transposition to her mom!

As soon as she opened the door, however, she got a surprise. At that time of day, her mother was supposed to be working at Simultech, so Will thought the apartment was empty. But there were voices coming from the living room!

"So, that's the deal," a man said.

Will froze. The man sounded a lot like her dad! What was he doing there?

"I should've guessed," a woman's voice replied. "After all these years, you haven't changed one bit."

That's Mom's voice, Will thought. Wait a second—Mom and Dad are talking. They're actually talking. That has to be a good thing! Right?

"I'll bet he's calling off the lawsuit," Will whispered to herself. "I'll bet he's going to work things out with my mom right now!"

Ever since she had heard about the custody hearing, Will had been feeling really torn up. The way her dad had broached the subject had been harsh . . . and mean. She had been holding out hope all along that her father was a good guy, and now it looked as though he really was! He had come to make up with them. Why else would he have been there, talking with her mom?

Trying to contain her excitement, Will took a deep breath. She had to see for herself. Quietly pushing her bedroom door open a few more inches, she peered carefully down the short hallway.

She saw her mother, Mrs. Vandom, pacing up and down the living room in a gray business suit. Will's father was sitting on the couch. Will couldn't see his face, but she recognized his long legs, crossed casually, with one big leather loafer lazily swinging back and forth.

Now Will was convinced that using transposition to get home had been a brilliant idea. She wouldn't have wanted to miss this! Things were going to work out! Her dad was going to withdraw his lawsuit. Her mom would forgive him. And then, maybe they could all be a family again!

With a hopeful heart, Will cocked an ear to listen closer. . . .

"I'm a consistent person, Susan," Will's father was saying in the living room. "Normally, that quality is appreciated."

Will liked what she was hearing so far. Her dad's tone sounded calm and reasonable. In fact, he sounded as if he were trying to sweet-talk her mother. Great!

But then her mom spoke up, and some of Will's happiness faded. "You're a lowlife, Thomas."

Will cringed. Her mother was still on the warpath. Not that Will blamed her entirely . . . After all, her father had served her with court papers.

"You gave me your word that you'd get out of my life *and* Will's life forever!" her mom railed, unaware of Will's silent hopes.

"That's a promise I would've gladly kept, dear," her dad replied. "But sometimes, life forces us to make difficult decisions. It wasn't easy for me to come here, but I promise you that after all this is over, you'll never see me again."

What is he talking about, Will wondered. What difficult decision has *he* had to make? And what does he mean, "never again"?

"Why should I believe that?" Will's mother asked.

"Because you have no choice," Mr. Vandom said. "Because I can take Will away from you. And believe me, I'm ready to do it."

No! Will thought. No! No! No! He's *still* threatening to take me away! I thought this talk meant no custody battle!

"This can't be happening," she whispered to herself, the hope in her heart beginning to sink.

"On the other hand," Will's father continued from his comfortable seat on the sofa. "I could withdraw my case and let you go back to your peaceful little life, and to your history teacher. As you can see, I'm serious. And now it's all up to you."

"I don't understand," Will's mother replied. "How is it all up to me? *You're* the one bringing the custody suit."

"I need money, Susan," Will's father explained. "A lot of money. Give me what I need and you can keep Will. But one false move, and I'll take your daughter away from you . . . and it'll be forever."

Will's eyes widened in horror at the same time that she heard her mother gasp.

"I told you, sweetheart. It's all up to you," her father repeated in a sickly sweet tone. "The choice is yours, dear, Will's fate is in your hands. I'm willing to withdraw my case and call off the custody trial—"

"If I *pay* you!" her mom shouted. "Aren't you ashamed of yourself, Thomas? You're asking me for money in exchange for Will, your own daughter!" In a voice of utter disgust, her mom asked, "How could you sink so low?"

Will stumbled backward into her room. "No," she whispered, "no . . ."

Stunned, she sank down onto the carpet. The situation with her father was worse than she had *ever* imagined. All along, Will had thought he was fighting *for* her, that he *wanted* her. But he didn't. He wanted to use her. Which meant that *everything* her father had done for her, given to her, or said to her had been part of a scheme!

From the day he'd come back into their lives, Thomas Vandom had been lying to Will.

He'd been pretending the whole time, just so he could blackmail Will's mom for money!

As tears filled her eyes and flowed down her cheeks, Will recalled the prophecy that Jewell had made. The old man—who had actually turned out to be a magical Water Shadow—had given Irma predictions about all of the Guardians—including Will. He had said that her father was going to make her suffer. Will had been determined not to believe Jewell, and even though she had helped save him from a gang of criminals, Will had never really opened up to the creature. But now it looked as though he had been telling the truth. Her father was making her suffer—big-time.

"Well, Susan," her father calmly continued, bringing Will back to the present, "I'd be flying much higher if certain deals of mine hadn't taken a turn for the worse."

"What deals?" Will's mother asked.

"I've got a major debt to pay off with some people who are getting impatient," Will's father said, "and you're my last chance."

"You're despicable, Thomas. Always the same old con artist. You make me sick."

"I had no choice," her father claimed. "You

never would've helped me of your own free will. All I needed to do was have you followed by a detective, my friend Harvey Slimerick, and the rest all fell into place on its own. First he took those photos of you with your dear Mr. Collins. And now, this . . ."

Now *what?* Will wondered. *Now what?*

She held her breath, listening for more, but things had become very quiet. Desperate to know what was happening, Will wiped away her tears and peeked around the edge of her bedroom door.

Her dad was now standing, with her mother close by, shuffling through a fat stack of photos. Suddenly, the look on Mrs. Vandom's face turned from surprise to fury.

Will wondered what could be in the photos. She didn't have to wonder long.

"You came out pretty well," her father said snidely. "You and your judge friend."

Judge friend? Will gasped. He must be talking about Judge Cook, she realized. Taranee's mother!

Will's mother put the photos down and glared at Will's father. "So what?" she said. "Theresa Cook is a friend of mine."

"If those pictures were made public she'd be taking a big risk. After all, it doesn't look good for a judge to be talking with someone whose case she is overseeing." Her father shrugged. "You decide what to do."

Will's father turned to the coatrack. He slipped his jacket off the hook and placed it over his arm. "If you give me what I'm asking for, those photos will disappear, along with my case."

"What?" Will's mother said in confusion. "You'll drop the case to take Will, just like that?"

Will's father waved his hand. "I'm not interested in getting custody of Will. I can easily leave her with you, but remember, it'll *cost* you."

Will's father walked over to a side table and picked up a pen. On the back of one of the private detective's photos he scribbled something down.

"You've got until noon tomorrow to think it over." He handed Will's mother the photo, pointing to what he'd just written on the back. "Here's my cell phone number, and beneath it is the amount I'm going to need."

Will's mother read the numbers. "This is

crazy!" she cried. "I don't have that kind of money."

"You're a resourceful woman, Susan," Will's father said. "You'll think of something."

He put on his jacket and headed for the door. Before he went out, however, he stopped and turned. "Remember," he warned, "you've got less than twenty-four hours. Noon tomorrow. Not a minute longer."

Slam!

With that, Will's father was gone. Still stunned, Will emerged from her bedroom. She needed to talk to her mother. But before she could take another step, the front door opened and closed again. *Slam!*

Will's mother had thrown on her coat and raced out of the house. Rushing to the window, Will looked out. A few moments later, her mother appeared far below, marching out of the building. She walked right to the curb, climbed into her car, and drove away.

Where is she going? Will wondered. To visit her bank for the money? Or to see her lawyer? Maybe she was going to warn Taranee's mother about the photos. Whatever she was doing, it wouldn't be fun. Will let out a big sigh. Neither of them should have to be dealing with such a nightmare.

Rubbing her throbbing temples, Will suddenly remembered the dream she'd had about her father. That should have been a warning. . . .

Decorative purple bunting had been draped all around a beautiful ballroom. Buffet tables were covered in white linen. Partygoers were dressed in eighteenth-century costumes. Women wore silk gowns. Men wore knee-high boots, breeches, and velvet coats. Everyone had powdered wigs on and held carved wooden masks over their faces.

As Will moved through the costume party, she ran into a tall, elegant woman. When the woman removed her blank wooden mask, Will recognized her. "Mom?" she said.

"I forbade you to come here!" Will's mother cried. A tall, broad-shouldered man stood next to her. He held a mask to his face, too, but it wasn't blank. This mask was different. It was carved with features that Will immediately recognized.

"Dad!" she exclaimed. "At least you—"

"Trust me, Will," her father said, cutting her off. "Trust me."

Will nodded as he removed the wooden mask. What he revealed underneath, however, wasn't a normal face. It was a featureless skull—the face of a monster.

Will had screamed herself awake that night. She'd sat straight up in bed, peering into the shadows of her dark bedroom and trying to reassure herself that what she'd experienced hadn't been real. It was only a dream, she'd told herself. It didn't mean *anything*.

Now she knew it had meant something.

Now Will knew the reason her mother had slapped her father's ring away that day. She knew why her mom refused to forgive her father and give him a second chance. At last, Will understood what her mother had known all along—her father *had been* wearing a mask for weeks. And today, for the first time, Will had seen what was underneath. She had seen the real Thomas Vandom.

He doesn't care about either of us, she thought. All he cares about is himself!

The realization was devastating. But for

some reason, Will wasn't totally shattered. A year ago, she might have been. But she'd changed a lot since she had moved to Heatherfield. Will had spent the last year of her life learning how to be a leader, to overcome her fears so she could stand and fight. With her friends by her side, Will had helped defeat the snake-man Cedric and his army, Frost the Hunter, the evil prince Phobos, and Nerissa, along with her dark beasts Khor and Shagon. They had even withstood a supernatural assault on their own friendship!

Now the enemy had arrived on Will's doorstep, and she needed to do something. She wasn't sure whose help her mom was seeking. But she did know who could help *her*. She reached for the phone.

"There's not a moment to lose," she whispered. And she began to dial.

EIGHT

Taranee walked through the main entrance to Heatherfield Park. The air was crisp, and all around her the trees were changing color.

It's amazing, she thought, peering through her round glasses. All summer long, these leaves were a uniform green. Then, in the fall, the temperatures plunged, and they were transformed, with each tree displaying its own unique color.

She couldn't help seeing W.I.T.C.H. the same way. On the outside, the girls all looked like typical middle-school girls. But when evil chilled their world, the Heart totally transformed them.

As she walked down the main path, Taranee imagined seeing W.I.T.C.H.'s energy streams swirling in the light fall breeze. There was Irma's blue water magic, Cornelia's green earth magic, Hay Lin's silver air magic . . .

And talk about *blazing* color, the fire Guardian thought, as deep scarlet and orange leaves fluttered down around her head. That's me, for sure!

Today Taranee had even dressed in flame-inspired colors. Her knitted cap was red and gold. And her pretty patchwork dress and belted coat were in shades of saffron. She'd worn matching beads in her single, shoulder-length braid. She smiled as she remembered how Nigel had put his arm around her between classes and played with the beads in her hair.

Strolling beneath the colorful fall canopy, Taranee sighed, with a feeling of quiet thanks. Nigel, like W.I.T.C.H., continued to be an important source of strength in her life. He was sweet and kind. Nigel was the first boy to appreciate and accept her for who she was— not for her "potential," or her perfect grades.

Taranee's first real date with him had happened the year before, on a snowy winter evening. He'd playfully started a snowball fight with her before they'd headed off to the movies.

Taranee looked forward to celebrating the anniversary of that first date—maybe with another snowball fight!

"Taranee! Over here!"

Taranee turned to see Hay Lin and Irma waving at her from a park bench. It was the spot where Will had asked them all to meet.

Waving back, Taranee quickened her steps to join the girls. Then Cornelia and Will arrived. As soon as she got there, Will began explaining why she'd called the emergency meeting.

As Will told them about her father's terrible plan, Taranee shuddered. She couldn't begin to understand how Will was feeling.

Imagine overhearing your dad trying to blackmail your mom—over your own custody! It would be beyond awful, Taranee thought.

Near the end of the story, Will mentioned her dad's private detective. She told them about the photos the man had taken.

Taranee tried to stifle a gasp.

"What is it?" Will asked, turning to face her friend.

"I already knew about it," Taranee admitted with a heavy sigh.

Will shook her head in confusion. "You

knew about the photos?" she asked.

"Not the photos," Taranee clarified. "I knew that my mom met with yours to warn her."

"Why didn't you tell me right away?" Will demanded. "I thought there weren't any secrets between us!"

"And there aren't," Taranee quickly assured Will. "But I was worried, and I didn't know what to do. I didn't want to mess things up more by saying anything."

Cornelia put a hand on Taranee's shoulder. "Well, your mom sure knew what to do."

Taranee nodded. "I'm proud of her. Even if I can still feel that slap she gave me."

While Taranee's recent problems with her mom didn't compare to what Will was going through, the past few weeks had been pretty harrowing in the Cook house.

As the memories came flooding back, Taranee brought her hand up to her cheek. The slap her mom had given her had caused a total war between them—and even now, she could feel the sting. The worst part was, Taranee had never seen it coming. The night it happened, everything had been going great.

She and Nigel had gone out with Hay Lin and Eric. It was—technically—Taranee's *first-ever* double date! The two couples had been going to check out the Rock and Roll Café in downtown Heatherfield. Unfortunately, they'd ended up at the police station, because of a run-in with Uriah.

Taranee had waited nervously for her mom to come and pick her up. She had hoped her mom would act like a judge—fair and reasonable. Instead, her mother had arrived seething with anger.

And then, just when Taranee thought it couldn't get worse, her mother had slapped her!

For Taranee, that had been the final straw. After trying so hard to be the perfect daughter, the perfect student, this was the thanks she got? An ugly, harsh slap of humiliation?

From that moment on, she'd gone on a total academic strike. Within a week, her school grades had plummeted. She'd purposely failed every pop quiz her teachers had given.

Of course, her mother had totally flipped. She'd ranted and raved, and, every day, she had picked Taranee up after school and delivered her to her new "study room." The room was her mother's home office, a paneled den lined with bookshelves.

It didn't matter where her mother put her. Taranee refused to do any homework. Instead, to pass the time, she had read her mother's legal files.

That was how Taranee had found out about the upcoming case against Will's mother. The file had fallen into her lap—literally. Within moments of opening it, she'd learned that Will's father was suing Will's mother.

My own mother is going to preside over a case that could change the life of my best friend, Taranee had realized at the time. And she never even bothered to *mention* it to me!

Soon after her discovery, Taranee had confronted her mother in the car. "You're about to put my friend's mother *on trial*."

"Oh, come on!" her mother had responded. "I'm a judge. Her file turned up on my desk, and I'm just doing my job."

"Fantastic!" Taranee had cried. "You'd rather believe all the mean things you hear from Will's dad, a guy you don't know anything about!"

"How . . . how dare you!" her mother had replied. "What would you know? You're just a child!"

Just a child? I may be just a child, Taranee had thought, but I know what my mother is doing. She's betraying friends in the name of her career. And it's wrong!

All of a sudden, Taranee had no longer been able to stand being *near* her mom. While the car was still moving, Taranee had yanked on the door handle.

"What do you think you're doing?" Taranee's mother had exclaimed. "Sit back in your seat right now!"

"No!" Taranee had shoved open the door and swung her legs out. Her mother had tried to hold her back. But Taranee's voice had become deadly serious. Her eyes blazed with a danger-ous warning. "Don't try to stop me, *ever* again. You've got no idea how much I've changed."

Taranee's outburst had had at least one good consequence. Her mother had gone to see Will's mother. She had shown her the legal file and the case against her. Plus, she'd warned her about the custody battle that was about to be waged by Thomas Vandom. Hidden from view, Taranee had witnessed the whole encounter.

Taranee was thrilled that her mother had done the right thing. She knew that her mom had put her job at risk. But doing the right thing sometimes meant getting into uncomfortable situations. If anyone knew that, the fire Guardian did!

"If my dad leaks those photos," Will warned Taranee, "your mom could be in serious trouble."

Taranee nodded, her thoughts jumping back to the crisis at hand. She knew that, of course. What she hadn't considered was what Hay Lin brought up next—"His blackmail scheme is a threat to all of us!"

Irma scratched her head and turned to Hay Lin. "How?"

"If Mr. Vandom doesn't get his money, he could win the lawsuit," Hay Lin explained. "Then Will would have to go with him and move away."

Taranee frowned. Hay Lin had a point. Without the Keeper of the Heart, their world wouldn't be the same.

"It would be the end of W.I.T.C.H.!" Hay Lin said. Her eyes were wide and panic-filled.

"You're right," Irma said. She frantically turned to Will. "It would be the end of everything!"

Will stood up. She put her hands on Irma's shoulders to steady her. "We're not down and out yet," she firmly reminded her.

"Will's right," Cornelia said. She adjusted her lilac beret and folded her arms over her matching jacket. "We can fix things. But this time, we've got to settle things with our own 'natural' powers."

Irma threw Cornelia a "duh" look. "Isn't that what we always do?"

Hay Lin ignored the two others and turned to their leader. "Have you got a plan, Will?"

"No." Will shook her head. "I want to stop my dad from getting away with this, but I don't know how."

The girls grew quiet as everyone tried to think of a solution. Will walked back and forth, kicking with her pink and black boots at the fallen leaves as she paced. Finally, she spoke again.

"We all have a weakness," she said. "And that goes for my dad, too. We just need to figure out what it is and how to use it against him."

Cornelia sighed. "But the problem is that we don't know him well enough to know what that weakness is."

Taranee watched as some of the hope in Will's eyes faded.

"Sure, *we* don't . . ." Hay Lin grinned, showing off her custom-designed braces. "But Kadma must know all about him!"

Taranee smiled. "Of course!"

Irma didn't get it. "Kadma?" she cried. "What does Kadma have to do with this?"

"It's simple," Hay Lin explained. "If the Rising Star Foundation watched over Will her whole life, Kadma must know everything about her."

"And about my family!" Will's grim face finally brightened. "Hay Lin's right!"

Taranee agreed. Hay Lin had come up with a great lead for them to follow. Kadma had been around for a very long time. Before she'd settled down in Fadden Hills to watch over Will, she'd been a Guardian. With her help, W.I.T.C.H. had a good chance of fighting back against Mr. Vandom.

"I'll go back to Fadden Hills and talk to her," Will declared.

Taranee stepped up. "And I'll go with you," she said. "My mother's future is riding on this, too."

Taranee wasn't looking forward to facing the cranky temper of the prickly Guardian. But she figured it was about time she put something on the line.

After all, if my mom can risk her career, she told herself, the least I can do is take a little trip to Will's old hometown!

NINE

"So, while Will and Taranee go off to find Kadma, what do *we* do?" Irma asked glumly. She collapsed on the cold park bench and shoved her hands into her coat pockets.

Clip-clop, clip-clop, clip-clop . . .

Irma noticed two police officers riding their horses down the park's main path. She felt just like those mounted cops: all dressed up for crime-fighting with no crime to fight!

She groaned, then said, "I don't want to sit around twiddling my thumbs!"

Cornelia rolled her eyes. "We'll take care of the *pictures*, Irma," she said, as though the answer were obvious.

The pictures? Irma thought. Oh, right! Of course!

91

Her mood picked up. She'd almost forgotten about the incriminating photos—the ones that the sleazy private detective had taken.

"Without those snapshots, his threats against Taranee's mom will burst like a soap bubble!" Cornelia cried excitedly.

Clip-clop, clip—

Irma froze. She noticed that the mounted cops had pulled up short to glance their way.

Nice going, Blondie, Irma thought. Why don't you shout "threats" a little louder. I don't think those cops heard you!

Irma glared at Cornelia and pointed to the police, who were now looking their way. *Keep your voice down,* she mouthed. Then she turned to the officers and gave them an innocent little wave. They glanced at each other before continuing down the path.

When the police were out of earshot, Hay Lin turned to Cornelia and Irma. "All we need to do is get our hands on the negatives," she said quietly. "If only we knew where to find them."

"Harvey Slimerick," Will told the girls. "Write that name down. That's the detective who worked for my dad. I heard him mention the name."

Hay Lin dutifully pulled a little sketch pad from her coat pocket and scribbled the name on a blank sheet of paper.

Ugh, Irma thought, what a creepy name. Still, she shook her head, the name alone wasn't enough to go on. She needed more information immediately. She started shooting questions at Will until the Keeper held up her hand to silence her.

"I don't know what he looks like or where he lives," Will insisted, "but the name's a good start."

Irma frowned. "A good start? What's so good about it?"

Irma's father was a policeman, so she knew what it took to track someone down. And from the sound of this guy's slimeball tactics, Irma doubted very much he was putting ads in the Yellow Pages. Creeps like Slimerick were underground operators. And they usually had a dozen aliases, too! One name wouldn't get the girls anywhere. They would need more.

Of course, Cornelia disagreed.

"Well, I think it's a great clue," Cornelia insisted, "for some of the finest investigative minds of our generation." She tipped back her lilac beret with her thumb like a smug know-it-all.

Irma rolled her eyes and stood up. "It's only a name, Corny! I don't know what I'll be able to do with it."

Cornelia smirked. "That's because *you* aren't one of the finest investigative minds of our generation!"

"Hey! My father's a policeman!" Irma shouted, moving so close to the earth Guardian that their noses were practically touching.

"So what?" Cornelia shot back, refusing to budge. "If my father was a pilot, would I know how to fly a plane?"

Irma was ready to scream. Cornelia sure had a short memory, she thought. After all, Irma was the one who had just solved the mystery of Jewell, the Water Shadow!

Irma had been the one to meet the man at the police station, and she'd figured out he was a supernatural being. He'd been trying to get back to his home in the sea, but some dangerous criminals had been intent on stopping him.

Okay, Irma admitted to herself, so maybe Cornelia helped me—especially with the computer research stuff. But I was the one who pushed W.I.T.C.H. into solving the mystery in the first place!

Irma was about to bring that up when Will rushed between them. "Calm down, guys!" she cried, separating them. "Right now we need to be *collaborating*, not fighting!"

Cornelia folded her arms and raised her pretty pointed chin in the chilly air. "I *am* collaborating," she insisted. "*She's* the one who's fighting."

"Try looking me in the eye when you say that!" Irma warned. Irma knew she was being extreme. But she couldn't help it! Cornelia had become a smugness factory, spewing out self-importance like polluted air!

Maybe it's my fault she's so full of herself, Irma thought. After all, I was the one who told her to take up ice-skating again. Now that Cornelia is back to competing in her favorite sport, she is also back to being as confident and bossy as she pleases!

Irma couldn't take all the credit for that, though. It was actually Jewell who had mentioned ice-skating. It was one of the several predictions he had made about the Guardians.

To Cornelia, he had suggested that she start

ice-skating again, and that that was the only way she would ever get over her broken heart. And it seemed to have worked. Cornelia told W.I.T.C.H. that ice-skating made her feel powerful and happy again. At last, she felt as if she were finally getting over Caleb.

And what thanks do I get for passing on the advice? Irma thought. *Smugitude.* Blondie's so busy being confident she forgot *I'm* part of the reason she feels good about herself again!

As Irma and Cornelia continued to argue, Will backed away. Within thirty seconds, Irma noticed her friend's retreat and quickly raised her hands in a *T,* for "time-out," to shush Cornelia.

"We've only got one day to do this," Will was now saying to Taranee and Hay Lin, apparently too tired to deal with the other girls' fighting. "By noon tomorrow, everything has to be settled."

"So let's not waste any more time," Taranee replied.

Irma crossed over to join Will.

"Are you sure it's okay if I come with you?" Taranee asked. "I know Kadma can be tough to take."

"Of course I want you to come," Will said,

resting a hand on Taranee's shoulder. "I'll need your warmth there with me. Fadden Hills is always cold this time of year!"

Before anyone could say more, a bright pink glow began to illuminate them. A moment later, the transposition was on!

Shaaaaa-zaaatz!

The brilliant pink light exploded in front of Irma. She stood staring at the empty space where two of her best friends had been only moments before.

Irma suddenly felt silly—and guilty—about fighting with Cornelia. Will and Taranee were totally backing each other up.

And we should be doing that, too, Irma thought. After all, Cornelia's never let me down . . . even though she *can* be a megapain some-times!

Sure, they saw things differently, but there was one thing they agreed on—helping Will. Plus, Irma had to admit that Cornelia had good ideas when it came to solving mysteries. And to help Will win this battle, they'd need every advantage.

Irma turned around and met the earth Guardian's eyes.

Okay, Blondie, Irma thought, we've argued enough for one day. Now, get off your high horse and let's figure out our next move. It's time we started cracking this case—*together!*

TEN

Shaaaaa-zaaatz!

Will opened her eyes. Heatherfield Park was gone, and so were the autumn leaves. Around her now was an endless scene of white.

"Wow, it's already snowing here," she whispered to Taranee, rubbing her arms. "Fadden Hills is even colder than I remembered!"

In front of her was a massive black gate adorned with elaborate, wrought-iron swirls. On either side of the gate were tall stone pillars, overgrown with vines. An engraved plaque that read RISING STAR FOUNDATION was displayed on one of the pillars.

Will took a deep breath and exchanged glances with the fire Guardian.

For some reason, Taranee wasn't

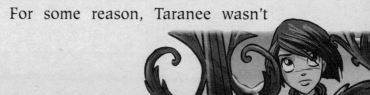

bothered by the snow. In fact, she was smiling at the frozen whiteness as if she were enjoying some secret, happy memory.

Probably about Nigel, Will figured. After all, those two had had that snowball fight on their first date! Taranee had just the kind of dreamy, romantic look on her face that Cornelia had used to get when she thought about Caleb. The look Will herself had once gotten on her face around Matt.

Will stopped herself from going any further with that depressing train of thought. She was about to ask Taranee what was up when her friend seemed to snap out of her momentary daydream, pointing to the black gate in front of them.

"Let's hope Kadma's at home," Taranee said. "I don't want to find out we've come all the way over here for nothing!"

"It was worth the trip, Taranee," Will assured her. "Kadma's inside."

Taranee pushed up her glasses. "How do you know?"

Will pointed to the top of the iron gate, where Kadma's blackbird, Cheepee, was perched.

Cheep-cheep-cheep!

Will knew that wherever Kadma went, Cheepee went. She also remembered that the bird doubled as the mansion's doorbell.

"Thanks to Cheepee," Will told Taranee, "Kadma now knows we're here!"

Moments later, the big gate creaked open, and Cheepee took off from his perch. He circled above the girls as they walked through the gate, then led them down a long, snow-covered path.

The two friends approached a huge mansion that featured marble columns and a grand, arched doorway. The building looked cold and hollow, like an empty shell. Will shivered as she marched toward it through the frozen powder in her knee-high boots.

Above, the blackbird's feathers stood out against the gray sky and the white snow below. Silently, the girls followed the bird inside and toward one wing of the mansion. Stepping through a tall door, they found themselves in an enormous greenhouse.

Taranee took a deep breath. "Wow," she murmured.

Will nodded, admiring the flowering plants, lush shrubs, and exotic fruit trees. She had been there before, but it was still an experience.

The smells were amazing: orange blossom, lavender, mint, rose, and honeysuckle.

Cheep-cheep-cheep!

Their feathered welcoming committee landed on a plant near a set of wicker chairs. Will waved to Taranee, and they walked over to the cozy collection of furniture and sank onto the cushioned seats.

Will noticed that Taranee looked a little freaked out, which was understandable. But Will wasn't worried. This weird place with its blackbird butler and greenhouse waiting room was oddly comforting. Tilting her head back, Will peered through the high, curved, transparent ceiling. Sunlight streamed down through the glass, warming the indoor garden, even in the middle of Fadden Hills's early winter.

Just then, a woman's voice said, "Hello." Will turned to find a slender older woman gliding toward them across the greenhouse floor.

It was hard to guess exactly how old Kadma was just by looking at her. The woman had a long black braid that was heavily threaded with silver. But her skin was flawless, with only the tiniest of wrinkles near her almond-shaped eyes. On this occasion she was wearing a lovely maroon gown with a high, straight collar. The edges were finely embroidered with gold.

She still looks amazing, Will thought, watching her approach. Not a day older than the last time I saw her . . .

Will knew that, despite her youthful appearance, Kadma had to be very old. She had once served as a Guardian alongside Hay Lin's grandmother, with the power of earth in her fingertips. But then, Kadma had made a mistake. She'd unleashed her temper on the Oracle. Because of that, Kadma was no longer permitted to enter Candracar. She was an outcast, the traumatic events of her past still echoing in her mind and making her bitter.

Will reminded herself not to bring up the topic of the Oracle or of Candracar. She also knew she had to be very polite with the former Guardian. Kadma demanded respect.

So, the first thing Will did was apologize for disturbing Kadma's privacy. The elderly woman accepted the apology and offered them some hot tea and cookies. In silence, Will sipped the delicious black tea and ate one almond cookie.

When a few moments had passed and Will felt she could speak, she got down to business.

"Did you know my father?" she asked Kadma, her voice jarringly loud in the quiet room.

Kadma nodded. "I know all about Thomas Vandom. When he left, you were only a few years old."

Good, Will thought, she does know! Which means, hopefully, she can give me some answers!

Will had been sure Kadma could help, for a very good reason. Years before, the Rising Star Foundation had placed people in Will's life to spy on her—to make sure no harm came to the future Keeper. Will had discovered this the last time she'd gone to Kadma's mansion. At first, she'd been horrified. Her entire childhood had felt like a lie. But now, she realized it had all been in her best interests. And, given her current situation, Kadma's knowledge was sure to be a help.

"Can you tell me about my father?" Will now asked Kadma.

Kadma paused before speaking, as though gathering her thoughts. "Your father has always lived in the world of business," she began. "He's an ambitious man, obsessed with wealth and success. His story is far too long to tell, and in any case, it wouldn't be anything new."

"My mom never wanted to talk about him," Will explained.

"Can you blame her?" Kadma furrowed her brow. "That man managed to turn her life into a living nightmare. . . ."

Will's hands gripped the arms of her wicker chair as Kadma's words sank in. The world felt as if it were shifting, and she needed to steady herself.

Taranee seemed to sense Will's discomfort and silently sent a warm glance her way. Will nodded, happy that the fire Guardian had come with her. This wasn't the kind of news she would have wanted to hear alone.

"Like many others," Kadma continued, "your father sacrificed the things dearest to him in the name of greed and egotism. Because of his actions, many people have suffered, which is why he's lost forever."

"But he wasn't always lost, was he?" Will asked, trying to imagine what had attracted her mom to someone like her dad in the first place.

"No," Kadma replied. "The man who married your mother was a very different person. It was his work that ended up distancing him from his family. Things were going well, but he wasn't happy. He began to make investments that were riskier and riskier. . . . Like some gamblers, Thomas practically became addicted to investing."

Will's mouth felt dry, and Kadma paused to let her pick up her delicate china cup. Uneasily, Will gulped down the black tea. Even though it wasn't easy to hear, Will wanted to know more. She nodded for Kadma to continue.

"The more money he earned, the more he lost," Kadma explained. "Your father found himself riding an endless roller coaster. He was moving constantly from great fortune to difficult times. . . ."

Kadma's voice trailed off as Will's mind filled up with long-repressed memories. At the time, Will had been too young to understand what was going on. But her mom must have known.

"What about my mom?" Will asked, setting down her teacup. "What did she do while my dad was risking the family's money?"

"She tried to help him," Kadma replied, "sacrificing all of her savings, right down to the very last cent. But Thomas wasn't satisfied.

He sold her parents' house without telling her. And, well . . ." Kadma paused as she put down her teacup. "The list of misdeeds is a long one.

"Susan had to manage on her own, making great sacrifices to hold on to what was left of her family," Kadma continued. "Your mother's a very strong woman, Will."

"I know," Will said, "but this time, all of her determination may not help her much."

"What do you mean?" Kadma asked.

Taking a deep breath, Will told Kadma the whole sorry story, from start to finish. She explained how her father had come back into their lives, how he had pretended to love her, when all along he was just trying to blackmail her mom. She talked and talked, letting it all pour out.

When she finally stopped, Kadma shook her head. "What you have told me is sad and terrible. . . ."

Taranee stood up. "That's why we're here, Kadma. We need your help."

Kadma closed her eyes. "I'm sorry to disappoint you, girls," she said softly, "but I can't do anything for you."

Oh, no, Will thought. No, no, no! This is what I was afraid of!

Will had figured Kadma might be reluctant to help them. After all, they reminded her of the life she had once led and had then lost. But she hadn't expected a total dismissal. She glanced at Taranee. The fire Guardian looked shocked.

"I feel no hostility toward you," Kadma assured them, opening her eyes again. "But I want nothing more to do with Candracar or its Guardians."

And with those words, the last of Will's hopes vanished.

ELEVEN

Kadma shook her head. It's too bad these girls wasted their time coming all the way out here, she thought. But I can't change the way I feel, and it's obvious they could never understand.

Will's big, expressive eyes blinked back tears of disappointment. And behind her round glasses, Taranee appeared both surprised and confused.

Perhaps if I explain, Kadma thought, then maybe they'll understand . . . and *go away*.

She sighed and turned to Will. "I had a task, and I completed it," she said firmly. "I watched over you and protected you up until the day you were told your fate. And when I gave you Halinor's diary, my mission was over."

Will's dejected expression was upsetting to see. Kadma turned away, focusing instead on one of the many exotic blossoms in her greenhouse. The vibrant red petals of the passion flower reminded her of the setting sun.

I'm a setting sun, too, Kadma thought. I have very little time left, and I don't wish to spend a moment of it remembering the past. It's just too painful. . . .

Once, Kadma had held the power of earth. She had had friends she thought she would never lose. In those youthful days, everything had been bright and new, full of budding promise.

We had the Power of Five, Kadma found herself recalling. Yan Lin, Cassidy, Nerissa, Halinor, and me . . . we were so happy and proud to be Guardians! Entrusted by the Oracle of Candracar with amazing abilities and responsibilities! The best part of all was that we were the best of friends . . . until that one dark and fateful day. . . .

The Oracle had summoned Nerissa to Candracar, for she had done the unthinkable. She had abused the power of the Heart. So the Oracle had taken the magic crystal away from

Nerissa and given it to a new Keeper—Cassidy.

The Oracle should have foreseen what would happen. After all, for years, Nerissa had carried the Heart inside her. She'd become attached to its power. When the Oracle ripped it away from her and gave it to Cassidy, that sent Nerissa over the edge.

Blinded by her need for the Heart, Nerissa lured Cassidy into a trap and did away with her.

Killing Cassidy had been a terrible, unthinkable act. The surviving Guardians were devastated. Nerissa had to be punished. Once again, she was brought back to Candracar—this time to stand trial for murder.

Kadma had watched Nerissa's trial along with Halinor and Yan Lin. In the end, the Oracle and the Congregation found Nerissa guilty. They sentenced her to imprisonment inside a remote volcanic mountain.

Even after all the years that had passed, Kadma could still hear the Oracle's chilling words, addressed to the Congregation of Candracar: *Nerissa shall be confined within the depths of Mount Thanos and deprived of her powers, with neither aid nor companionship. That is our decision!*

Yan Lin accepted the situation. Kadma and Halinor did not. Angrily, the two Guardians stepped forward. They accused the Oracle of having let the whole thing happen in the first place.

He had given the Heart to Cassidy, but, in doing so, the Oracle should have known how crazed Nerissa would become, they thought. He should also have known she was capable of killing Cassidy over it. He should have seen it coming and intervened to stop it!

The usually calm and collected Oracle had reacted harshly to Kadma and Halinor's charges. He declared that because they refused to accept his choice and Nerissa's destiny, they would never again be allowed in Candracar; they would never again have a place in the Congregation, and they would *always* be out-casts.

Crushed by the Oracle's harsh decree, Kadma and Halinor had returned to Earth. But they had not severed *all* their ties to their past. Together they established their Rising Star Foundation in memory of their beloved lost friend, Cassidy. They'd raised and educated orphans. And some of those orphans had ended up watching over Will Vandom, the girl destined to be the next Keeper of the Heart.

Sadly, Halinor had passed away before she could meet the new Keeper. When Will needed it most, however, Kadma had given her Halinor's diary. It had helped Will find Cassidy's Star and the Heart when it was once again threatened—and even stolen—by Nerissa.

A short time after, the new Guardians had gotten rid of Nerissa once and for all, which meant that Will was safe. Kadma felt that her obligations were fulfilled—and *finished*.

"The Rising Star Foundation will continue to help those who are in need and unable to help themselves," Kadma said now to the girls. "But I can't do anything to help you. You have the power to work things out on your own."

Kadma had said all she was going to say. Turning to bid the girls good-bye, however, she found herself facing an angry fire Guardian itching for a fight.

"How can you just stand there and do nothing?" Taranee raged, her brown eyes blazing. "If Will has to leave Heatherfield, what will become of W.I.T.C.H.?"

Kadma sighed. Taranee's temper was touching in a way. It reminded her of her own youthful passion. But Kadma had no time for it now. "This might surprise you, Taranee," she calmly replied, "but what becomes of W.I.T.C.H. doesn't concern me in the least."

The fire Guardian's mouth fell open. "What?" She shook her head as if Kadma had spoken words in an unrecognizable language. "You . . . you . . ."

Taranee took a step forward, and Kadma's eyes narrowed. She was losing her patience with the girl.

"Thanks, Kadma. You've been really helpful," Will said, grabbing Taranee's arm and pulling her away. "I'm sorry if we've disturbed you."

"Wha . . . ?" Taranee stared in confusion at her friend. "Why are you apologizing?"

"It's time to go, Taranee!" Will insisted. "There's nothing else we can do here."

Will extended two fingers, calling up a piece of the power living inside her. Kadma gasped as she saw and felt the familiar dazzling energy that had once transformed her.

The young Guardians stared into the pink

light. The Heart of Candracar glowed brighter, and then . . .

Shaaaaa-zaaatz!

In a single, blinding flash, the girls were gone.

For a moment, after the spectacular light died out, Kadma regretted sending them away. In her head, she could almost hear her beloved friend Halinor's voice scolding her: *I'm ashamed of you! Is this how you think Cassidy or I would have treated young Guardians in need of help? Are you so lost in your own self-pity that you've forgotten what it's like to be a friend?*

Even Cheepee seemed to be taking the girls' side.

Cheep-cheep-cheep! The bird squawked at Kadma as she stood alone in the middle of the greenhouse.

"I don't owe anyone anything, Cheepee!" Kadma snapped in reply.

Helping those girls would be almost like helping the Oracle, she thought. But all those years ago, he *neglected* to help Cassidy! He had the power to prevent Nerissa from killing Cassidy, yet he didn't do a thing! So why should I do anything now?

Turning away from her cheeping blackbird, Kadma left the warm, sunny greenhouse.

"I don't owe anybody anything!" Her voice echoed in the hallway of the vast, hollow mansion. *"Anything!"*

TWELVE

Back in Heatherfield, Irma, Cornelia, and Hay Lin approached the police station. Ducking behind a car, Irma caught sight of an officer talking to his prisoner.

"Nice tattoo, Stromberg," the cop remarked to the big, hairy thug.

"Gee, thanks," said the handcuffed thug as he climbed out of the police car.

"Is it new?" the officer asked, walking his prisoner toward the station house. "You didn't have it the last time you got put away. . . ."

Since Irma's father was a policeman, this sort of scene was nothing new to her. She'd seen a hundred like it. Hay Lin, on the other hand, stood gaping in horror.

"Check out that ugly mug!" Hay Lin whispered, pointing to the big, hairy criminal.

Irma stifled a giggle at the sight of the air Guardian's expression. Hay Lin was gawking at the routine "perp walk" like it was some sort of weird circus act.

Oh, well, Irma thought, I guess I can't blame her. I mean, Hay Lin's dad runs a Chinese restaurant. Tattooed criminals in handcuffs aren't exactly a part of *his* business routine!

"Why did we come here?" Hay Lin groaned.

Irma rolled her eyes.

"We came here to find our friend Slimerick," Cornelia reminded Hay Lin. "All private investigators have to get their licenses registered with the police."

"I don't think they'll just hand us the information we're looking for," Hay Lin said.

It was more than clear to Irma that Hay Lin didn't like being there. And Irma wasn't surprised. The last time the air Guardian had been inside the Heatherfield police station, she'd been under arrest, along with her boyfriend, Taranee, and Nigel!

"Don't worry," Irma said. "If they won't give

it to us, we'll just go find it ourselves. Leave it to me."

"What are you going to do?" Cornelia asked.

Irma grinned. "Just wait and see."

The water Guardian closed her eyes and concentrated. She hadn't done this in a while, so it felt a little strange. Still, she was determined. As the magic inside her began to hum, she felt her skin start to tingle. And then it happened.

Kziiiiin!

She disappeared.

"Irma!" Cornelia whispered. "Are you nuts? Somebody might see you!"

"How could they? I'm invisible," Irma pointed out, laughing when she saw her friends vainly trying to figure out where she was standing.

The magic was a kind of force field surrounding her. Anything she wore or picked up would enter the field and become invisible, too.

"You can't be serious!" Cornelia warned. "This is your big plan?"

Ignoring her, Irma walked right toward the front door of the police station.

Cornelia moved to the spot where Irma had been. She flailed around with her hands. But she couldn't feel Irma's body, because Irma was gone!

"Get back here!" Cornelia cried softly.

Irma rolled her eyes and kept walking. Corny's really got to learn how to chill, she thought, stepping into the station house lobby.

Irma knew, however, that Cornelia had reason to be worried. Becoming invisible had its dangers. She remembered the time Will turned invisible during the Karmilla concert at the Futuredome in Heatherfield.

A portal to Meridian had opened up beneath the arena. Invisible, Will had snuck into the Futuredome's basement to investigate. What she'd found was Cedric, Phobos's second in command. Unfortunately, she'd been carrying her dormouse with her, and, at the worst possible moment, it had leaped from her arms. Once the critter was out of Will's force field, it became visible again, which meant that Cedric almost caught Will!

Luckily, Will and her pet escaped, but it had been a close call. Today, though, Irma wasn't carrying a dormouse with her—or any other small mammal! So she figured she already had an advantage.

Inside, the lobby was crowded with cops and civilians. Invisible Irma immediately stepped to the right to avoid an old man. Then she jumped to her left to dodge a policewoman. And then she went right again to avoid a direct hit from the big tattooed thug she'd seen earlier outside!

Yikes! Irma thought. Being invisible is harder than it is fun. It's so difficult to avoid bumping into people around you!

Carefully, she made her way to a space behind the front counter. There were lots of hallways in the station, and Irma knew them well. Her dad's office wasn't hard to find. But she had to be extra cautious as the cops brushed by her.

Look out, she thought, moving away from the counter, invisible girl coming through!

Finally, she reached a familiar door. The desk inside was vacant.

Hmmm, Irma thought, this is a good sign. Dad's not in his office, but his computer's up and running!

She sat down at her dad's desk. The screen was easy to figure out; she was able to access the police records with a few clicks of the mouse.

I hope he won't get too angry if I run a quick search, she thought. After all, it's just a matter of looking up one name so I can find an address.

Irma typed the investigator's name into the search engine: *Slimerick, Harvey*.

Seconds later, a page came up with the man's name at the top. Irma read the screen. There was information about his private-eye license, and—

Bingo! she thought. His office address!

"Well, well, well," she murmured to herself as she jotted down the street number, "seems our creepy private eye doesn't live in Heatherfield proper. But he's certainly close enough!"

"Beautiful Hutchville!" Irma exclaimed as the girls stepped off the bus some forty minutes later. After leaving the station, Irma had found her friends waiting. She had quickly turned herself visible again and then filled them in on what she had discovered. With the address in hand, they had grabbed the next bus and headed out in search of Harvey Slimerick. Now, looking around her, Irma added, "The oh-so-cheerful outskirts of Heatherfield."

Of course, she was joking. Hutchville was the gritty factory town. The buildings were crumbling, the sidewalks were cracked, and trash littered the streets. In Irma's opinion, Hutchville was about as cheerful as Mrs. Knickerbocker's detention room.

With a map in their hands, the girls tracked down Harvey Slimerick's address. They turned the corner and approached a run-down row house. A burned-out car was parked in front of it.

Cornelia shuddered. "This is just the kind of place where you'd expect to find a guy like Slimerick."

Irma laughed. "Not everyone can afford a penthouse like yours, Corny, darling, but I'm sure the sleazebag deserves a rat hole like this."

And "rat hole" was putting it nicely. The first-floor windows of the structure were boarded up, and there was a big "For Sale" sign on the scarred front door.

"His office is on the third floor." Hay Lin pointed to one of the windows. It was closed, but at least it wasn't boarded up.

"Let's go through the alley," suggested Hay

Lin. "That way, nobody will see us."

Irma and Cornelia nodded in agreement.

The girls crept around the building. In the shadows of the deserted alley, they all stared up at the third floor.

How are we going to get up there? Irma wondered.

As if reading her thoughts, Hay Lin giggled and closed her eyes. Silver air magic streamed around her and began to spin.

Cornelia and Irma stepped back.

"Here I go!" Hay Lin said, commanding the wind to lift her up, up, up.

When she got to the window, she lifted the rickety frame and peered inside. "It's perfect," she softly called down to them. "No one's home. The coast is clear, guys!"

Irma watched Hay Lin climb through the window.

As the water Guardian, Irma certainly could have tapped a hydrant and ridden a spout of water up after her, but it was a chilly day, and she wasn't in the mood to get wet. So when Hay Lin stuck her head back out, Irma called, "Help us get up there!"

Hay Lin nodded and stirred the air once

more for her friends. In no time, Irma and Cornelia were being lifted to the third-floor window, too. They all climbed through. But once inside, none of them were very happy to be there.

Ugh, Irma thought as she looked around. This office is disgusting!

Boxes and papers were scattered all over the room. The paint on the walls was peeling, and the trash can on the dirty carpet was filled to overflowing. A pizza box with a few rock-hard slices left in it sat on the desk, and paper cups and empty soda bottles littered the floor.

"Looks like a real pigsty!" Hay Lin cried.

Irma pinched her nose. "It smells like one, too!" she declared in a nasal voice. "A family of wet dogs would smell like a rose garden by comparison!" To make her point, she ran to the front window. The frame was sticky, but she managed to force it wide open. "Air!" she cried, releasing her nose and gasping for a fresh lungful of oxygen.

Cornelia ignored her theatrics. "Those photos have got to be here somewhere in the middle of this mess!" she insisted. "Let's get to work, guys . . . because time's running out."

Irma sighed. Cornelia wasn't kidding. Will's deadline was noon the following day. If they didn't come up with something to help her mom, the custody battle would go forward.

Irma hated working in a garbage dump, but they had no choice. Will needed their help!

It seemed to them all that the best place to start was the detective's files. A banged-up metal filing cabinet stood in the corner. It was stuffed with yellowing folders. But like everything else in the office, they were a complete mess. They weren't in alphabetical order, and all of them were overflowing.

To make matters worse, there were stacks of boxes filled with more folders all over the room, and the desk and threadbare sofa were covered with piles of papers.

Cornelia took charge and ordered each of the girls into a different section of the room. Irma bristled at Corny's bossy attitude, but she didn't argue. There wasn't any time for fighting. Various signs pointed to the fact that the private eye had been there recently: a lamp was burning in the corner, and a coffeemaker had been left on.

Slimerick could come back at any time,

Irma realized. So they really did have to work fast!

Twenty minutes later, Cornelia let out a big sigh. "Find anything?" she asked.

"Nothing," Irma replied in frustration. She'd rifled through boxes and boxes of file folders. None had contained anything about Will, her mom, or Judge Cook.

"Nothing here, either!" Hay Lin called from her spot beside an open drawer of the metal file cabinet.

Irma scratched her head. "Maybe he kept the photos locked up in a safe or hidden somewhere else," she suggested.

"Let's hope not," Cornelia replied.

Thump . . . thump . . . thump . . .

At the sound of heavy footsteps, Irma froze. So did Cornelia and Hay Lin. Someone was coming up the staircase! The girls exchanged worried glances.

What do we do? Irma wondered, her heart beginning to pound faster.

Seconds later, the office door burst open so hard it slammed against the back wall.

"Hold it right there!" a man cried.

He had greasy hair and a thin mustache. A

stained, wrinkled trench coat hung from his skinny frame. He wouldn't have been all that scary, except that he was holding a gun, and his finger was on the trigger.

"Huh?" he mumbled, lowering the weapon as he looked around. "But . . . there's nobody here. . . ."

Oh, yes, there is, silly man, Irma thought. There are three of us here! You just don't know where to look.

And for good reason! The girls were upside down, their feet magically sticking to the ceiling. Irma, Cornelia, and Hay Lin were as good as invisible!

Irma jerked her thumb toward the open door. Hay Lin and Cornelia understood the gesture and nodded. Together the girls used the ceiling as a floor and walked right out the door!

Behind them, the private eye shook his head, looking under his desk and inside his closet. "But the front window is open. . . . I didn't leave it like that. . . . And I was sure I heard someone in here," he mumbled in frustration.

Back out on the sidewalk, Irma took a deep breath of fresh air. That was close!

She was glad they had gotten out of there without getting hurt! But she was sorry they'd come away empty-handed. If the photos of Will's mother were in that disaster of an office, Irma had no idea how to find them.

"So, what do we tell Will?" Hay Lin asked as they walked away.

We tell her the truth, Irma thought in frustration. We tell her we failed.

THIRTEEN

"You did everything you could, guys," Will told her friends the next day, "and I really appreciate it."

The Guardians had gathered in Will's bedroom. Cornelia and Hay Lin sat on her bed, Irma sat cross-legged on the floor, and Taranee was leaning against Will's desk.

Will, meanwhile, paced the room, trying to stay calm.

After everything they'd done, the incriminating photos were still in the hands of Will's father. And that meant he still had the upper hand. He could still blackmail Will's mom and Judge Cook. He could still win the custody case and take Will away from her mother and her best friends.

"It's five minutes to twelve," Cornelia noted, glancing at her wristwatch. "What happens now?"

Suddenly, the five girls heard the creak of hinges as the front door opened.

A confused expression on her face, Will raced across the carpet and opened the door of her bedroom a crack. Her mother was walking into the apartment.

Will moved quickly out into the hallway, shutting the door behind her. "Mom!" Will called.

Her mother looked surprised to find Will at home, and Will had expected as much. Thanks to a little transposition, she'd snuck out at lunch period—and taken her friends with her. They had needed a quiet place to fill each other in on the previous day's events.

"Shouldn't you be at school?" Will's mom asked.

Will nervously scratched her head. "We got out early. There was, um, a teacher's strike . . . or something like that."

Her mom looked at her skeptically.

"And why aren't *you* at work?" Will asked, turning the tables on her mother.

For a second Will's mom had no answer. Then she lifted an eyebrow and said, "There was a strike . . . or something like that."

"There was a strike? Or something like that?" Will repeated. "Isn't that my line?"

A smile tugged at the corners of Mrs. Vandom's mouth. But it was not enough to erase the sadness in her eyes.

For as long as Will could remember, she had seen her mother the same way—as a polished, together woman. It had never occurred to her that her mom might have real problems, or that not everything was rosy and perfect.

Thanks to Kadma, Will now understood how much her mother had been through. For years, while her dad had risked all their money, her mom had been pretty much powerless.

She must have felt so scared and alone, Will thought. So frustrated and helpless—exactly the way I felt when I learned about my destiny as Keeper of the Heart.

Yet, despite all of the hardships, Will's mom had made it through, and protected her daughter, too. Tears welled up in Will's eyes. She was incredibly proud of her mother. She didn't want to leave her! She didn't want her con-artist father to take her away!

She opened her mouth to say just that, but her mother spoke up first.

"Why don't you go back to your room now, Will," her mom gently suggested. "I'm expecting a call. . . ."

Will nodded and slowly walked back into her bedroom. Shutting the door behind her, she struggled to hold back the tears.

For a moment there was silence. "What did your mom decide to do?" Taranee finally asked quietly.

"I don't know," Will whispered, "but whatever it is, I trust her." She resumed pacing across her bedroom carpet. It was exactly noon. She remembered her father's warning to her mother the day before: *Remember, you've got less than twenty-four hours. Noon tomorrow. Not a minute longer.*

The Guardians all looked tense. After five minutes, Will couldn't take it anymore. She opened the bedroom door again and peeked into the living room.

Her mother was sitting stiffly on the couch. She was staring at the phone, waiting for it to ring. "Come on, Thomas, call," Will heard her mother murmur. "I'm ready for you. . . . I want you to know that I'm *not* afraid of you."

Will stepped a little farther out of her bedroom. She now had a better view of the living room, but there was nobody there besides her mom, who was simply practicing the speech she was going to give her father.

"I won't give in to your blackmail, Thomas," her mom continued quietly. "And you'll never get Will."

Riiiiiiiiiinnnggg!

Will's mother snatched up the receiver before it could ring again. "Hello?" Dead silence followed as she listened to the person on the other end of the phone. "Yes?" she said. "Really?"

For some strange reason, her voice didn't sound upset or angry. In fact, to Will's ears, it sounded surprised and even *happy.*

Will stepped all the way into the hall. Her mother was smiling.

"I see . . ." her mother said into the phone. She listened some more and finally said, "Thank you!" Slowly, she hung up the phone.

Will entered the living room. "Who was that?" she asked.

"It was Judge Cook, honey!" Mrs. Vandom exclaimed. "She was calling from the courthouse with great news! Five minutes ago, your father withdrew his case!"

Omigosh! Will thought. It's over! He's dropped the lawsuit! "Yahoo!" she shouted.

Behind her, the Guardians peeked out from the bedroom. Will saw them and beckoned to them. Will's mom looked startled to see all of Will's friends in the house, but she didn't say anything. When everyone was gathered in the living room, Will shared the good news; the girls whistled, screamed, and jumped up and down.

"So what happened?" Will asked after they'd all screamed themselves silly and finally calmed down. "He changed his mind, just like that?"

"I don't know how it happened," Will's mom said. She grinned. "All I know is that it's *wonderful*!"

Just then, Will heard a light tapping on the windowpane.

Toc-toc-toc . . .

It was a bird!

Will stepped closer to the window, and her

eyes widened. It wasn't just any bird, it was a blackbird.

"Cheepee!" she cried.

She waved the Guardians over and pointed to Kadma's beloved pet. They all gasped and looked at one another in disbelief.

Will knew they were all wondering the same thing—what was Kadma's bird doing there?

FOURTEEN

From the backseat of her limousine, Kadma
fixed her gaze on the courthouse doors. When
a tall redheaded man emerged, she recognized
him immediately. It wasn't difficult. For years,
Kadma had watched Thomas Vandom ruin his
family.

As he descended the white stone staircase,
Vandom noticed the limousine and straight-
ened his tie. He approached Kadma's driver.

Without a word, the driver, Perkins, opened
the back door. Vandom bent down to peer
inside, his eyes darting back and forth.

Kadma met his nervous eyes. "Is it all taken
care of, Mr. Vandom?" she asked.

"Yup, all taken care of!" he assured her
in a silky, singsong voice.

Kadma didn't care for the man's slimy manner. She would have preferred to be anywhere but there next to him. Nevertheless, there was business to conclude. She waved him into the car and tried not to cringe as he sank into the soft leather seat. As soon as he was seated, Perkins shut the door.

"This is yours, then," she told him, holding out a check.

Like a starving man seeing a slice of bread, Vandom seized the slip of paper.

"As you see," Kadma said, "the amount is greater than what you needed."

Vandom's gaze ran across the numbers. His eyes widened in delight.

"Consider it a little incentive," Kadma said pointedly, "to get completely *out* of the picture *once and for all*."

Mr. Vandom laughed. "You can count on it, lady!" He pocketed the small fortune. "I don't know who you are or why you're doing all of this, but I'm outta here! Promise." He reached for the door handle and exited the limousine. Perkins immediately stepped forward and shut the door behind him.

Before the red-haired man could get too far,

Kadma rolled down the window. "And don't forget, Mr. Vandom," she called, "I'll be keeping my eye on you."

Mr. Vandom raised an eyebrow, but he said nothing. Turning once more, he began to walk away just as his cell phone rang.

Breep! . . . Breep! . . . Breep!

From inside the limousine, Kadma cocked an ear. She was close enough to make out the conversation and eager to hear what he was going to say—and to whom.

"Hey, there, Slimerick," Mr. Vandom said into his phone. "Huh? Oh, of course . . . the rest of your money! Sorry, buddy, but the plans have changed a bit. Your pictures won't be needed anymore, which means I don't owe you a thing!"

He snapped his cell phone shut. *Click!* Almost immediately, it rang again.

Breep! . . . Breep! . . . Breep!

Mr. Vandom laughed. "Go ahead and ring!" he said. "But I don't feel like talking to you."

Vandom threw his phone right into a nearby trash can.

Breep! . . . Breep! . . . Breep!
Breep! . . . Breep! . . . Breep!

The phone kept ringing as he walked away.

From the backseat of her limo, Kadma exhaled in relief. "We can go now, Perkins," she said to the man.

Perkins nodded. As he pulled away from the curb, Kadma considered how happy the young Keeper probably was at that moment—along with the other young Guardians.

Kadma thought of her own old friends, Halinor and Cassidy. Wherever they were in the cosmos, she hoped they were happy, too.

Just then, she heard a familiar sound.

Cheep-cheep-cheep!

Her blackbird was flying by her car. When they reached the corner, she rolled down her window once again.

"Happy now, Cheepee?" she asked her loyal pet. He ought to be, she thought. *He wouldn't stop chirping until I did something to help those girls!*

I said I wasn't going to get involved in this, Kadma thought with a little smile. *I wasn't going to help Will, because the Oracle didn't help Cassidy. But then I would have been behaving just like the Oracle, and I would* never want to do that—*ever*. But now, my job is truly done.

Cheep-cheep-cheep!

"Fine, fine," Kadma told the little blackbird. "Let's go home."

FIFTEEN

Breep! . . . Breep! . . . Breep!

Again and again Will watched her mother try to call her dad. She could hear the little electronic beeping on the other end of the line, but he never picked up.

"He's not answering," her mother said, shaking her head. Finally giving up, she switched off the phone. "Another disappearance with no explanation!"

"Weird," Will said.

Will's mom shrugged. "You know what I say? It's all for the best!"

Will exchanged glances with Cornelia, Taranee, Hay Lin, and Irma. They were grinning.

"We did it, Will!" her mom cried.

"I know! I can't believe it! How do you feel?" Will asked.

"It's like starting life all over again!" Mrs. Vandom cried. "It's . . . it's wonderful!"

It *is* wonderful, Will thought.

Thomas Vandom and his threats were out of their lives. Because of Cheepee's little visit, Will knew that Kadma had come through for them. Somehow, the old Guardian had found a way to keep the new Guardians together.

Her mother opened her arms, and Will stepped into them for the greatest hug of her life. And when Will's mom let go, W.I.T.C.H. was right there, waiting.

Irma, Cornelia, Taranee, and Hay Lin all stepped up. Giggling with joy, the five girls hugged. The magic stretched among them like an invisible ribbon binding them together. Will could feel each of their elemental streams.

Water!

Fire!

Earth

Air!

Safe in her circle of friends, Will let out a huge sigh.

We've come a long way, she thought, every

one of us. The journey we've taken this past year has been the most important of our lives. The most rewarding.

Will knew there were probably more changes in store for them—and challenges, too. But no matter what the situation, Will knew she could always count on her friends, just as they could count on her.

As long as the Power of Five sticks together, Will told herself, we can't fail! After all, working together, we saved the world. Working together, we saved each other. And as long as we *keep* working together, there's nothing we can't fight. There's nothing we can't accomplish, because . . .

We are powerful!

We are magical!

We are united!

We are . . . W.I.T.C.H.!

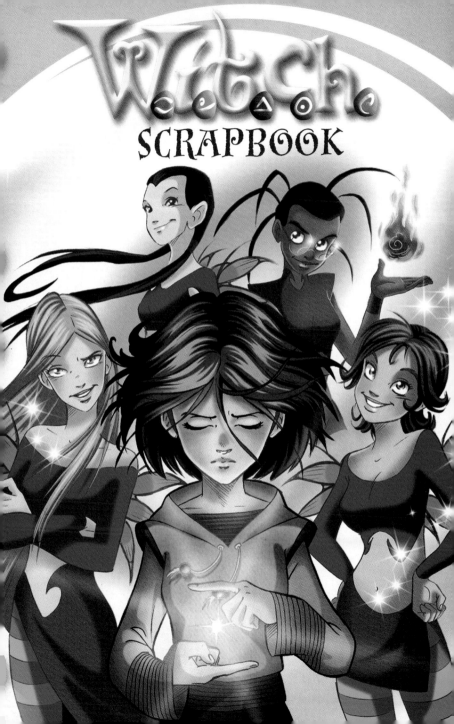

Isn't Nigel the dreamiest? I'm so lucky—h_ likes me for who I am (and doesn't mind that my friends come first)!

Peter always helps me out in a pinch.

Taranee

Will and I clicked from the very first day of school. Her ♥ is as big as the Heart of Candracar!

I'll never forget Caleb.
How could I? First loves are
the deepest..

Cornelia

Elyon may be a
queen now, but
she has always
been one of my
best friends.

I always knew my grandma was strong—I just never knew she was Guardian strong!

SKETCHBOOK

Hay Lin

Will and I may be different, but that only makes our friendship stronger.

We're five friends with
the power to save the world . . .
and each other!

The power of true
friendship never ends.